MW00761614

AMERILAND

By

Melody Kay Danals

© Copyright 2003 Melody Kay Danals. All rights reserved.

No part of this publication may be reproduced, stored in a retrieval system, or transmitted, in any form or by any means, electronic, mechanical, photocopying, recording, or otherwise, without the written prior permission of the author.

Printed in Victoria, Canada

National Library of Canada Cataloguing in Publication

Danals, Melody Kay
     Ameriland / Melody Kay Danals.

ISBN 1-55395-757-1

    I. Title.

PS3604.A52A74 2003   813'.6   C2003-900598-4

TRAFFORD

This book was published *on-demand* in cooperation with Trafford Publishing. On-demand publishing is a unique process and service of making a book available for retail sale to the public taking advantage of on-demand manufacturing and Internet marketing. **On-demand publishing** includes promotions, retail sales, manufacturing, order fulfilment, accounting and collecting royalties on behalf of the author.

Suite 6E, 2333 Government St., Victoria, B.C. V8T 4P4, CANADA

Phone	250-383-6864	Toll-free	1-888-232-4444 (Canada & US)
Fax	250-383-6804	E-mail	sales@trafford.com
Web site	www.trafford.com	TRAFFORD PUBLISHING IS A DIVISION OF TRAFFORD

HOLDINGS LTD.

Trafford Catalogue #03-0120   www.trafford.com/robots/03-0120.html

10   9   8   7   6   5   4   3   2

This book is for my boys
Nathan, Andrew and Stephen.

And all things, whatsoever ye shall ask in prayer, believing, ye shall receive.

Matthew 21:22

Acknowledgements

To my husband Ken who helped put this book together.

To my great friend, Barbara Hester, who read every word and encouraged me along the way with praise and prayer.

To my mother-in law JoAnn Collins, who also read the book and did the editing for me.

To my good friends John and Paula Fayad, who gave me good advice along the way.

To my parents, Charlie and Eula Langford, who always have been inspirations to all the children, grandchildren and great-grandchildren.

History

Ameriland was known as "Gudow" by the natives of the planet. It was discovered by American space travelers in the year 3000. There were few differences in the characteristics of the Gudows and the American Earthlings. Gudows have one extra finger on each hand and an extra toe on each foot. They are tall with dark features. They were a peaceful race and easy to colonize.

In the early 3000's missionaries converted them to the Christian faith. Earthmen began to marry and mix with the Gudows. They had tradition and culture that they had wanted to preserve, and passed laws to prevent the mixing of the races. This went on for years until the Americans made Gudow an American colony and thus named the new land "Ameriland." They lived side by side for years and begin to marry each other again, and soon the name "Gudows" was replaced with the name "Amerilanders."

Ameriland became a space center of exploration. Schools were built and the education was good. Americans, looking for a good living and peaceful place to raise a family, flocked to this new land. It took months to get there at first, but the time had been shortened with new ways of space travel.

Ameriland is a paradise, with lush greenery and flowering plants. It is tropical on most of the planet, with steady temperatures. There are no seasons and there are two small suns and a beautiful luminous moon. It never gets completely dark in the southern part of the planet, where most of the colonization took place.

Russo, a nearby planet, was known as "Lahid" by the natives of that planet. The planet was discovered by the earthlings from Russia. There are two types of natives on opposite sides of this small planet. The Talcots, who live to the north on the best land, have three eyes and are a large warring tribe. The Canots live to the south. They have slanted eyes and are a much more advanced tribe. When the Russians landed, they also mixed with the people.

Russia, not wanting to be outdone by the Americans, colonized the planet and named it "Russo." Colonizing this planet did not go as well as the Ameriland planet. They were always warring over territory. Some of the Talcots and the Canots had traveled to

Ameriland to escape the disputes and to have a better life. The Talcots found an area much like back home in the "Cavhill" territory on Ameriland. They tried to make a living there and live among the natives of that area, but it proved to be a failure. Some moved back to Russo, others moved to the south side of Ameriland. Russo was never completely at peace, but they lived and worked together for hundreds of years.

The Gallagers

Reeny was the first born son of the Gallagers. Even as he lay on his mother's chest right after birth, he gave his parents the once over. There was something in his eyes that caused his parents to believe this was no ordinary child. He turned over a few hours after birth, which caused the nurses some grief. The little boxed crib seemed too confining to this small bundle of energy. The nurses waved "good-bye" happily to the Gallagers as they left the hospital.

Maxwell followed his brother into the world two years later. Max was a good baby and seldom cried. Reeny, however, made sure he cried quite often. Max came into the world happy and he did not take life too seriously.

Luke Christian Gallager was born five years after Max. Luke was more in appearance like his brother Reeny, but had more of a personality like Max. Luke was resilient and strong. These attributes proved just what he needed with the future he faced. Even in the year 3300, dyslexia was an obstacle to overcome. Diagnosed early, he had adapted well and was becoming quite an artist.

Each of the Gallagers marched to a different drum. This proved overwhelming to their mother, Kay, who as a general rule was a quiet person. A small woman, but somewhat attractive, she went about her life teaching Kindergarten and trying to keep her boys in line. Their dad, Vincent, however was not known for his quiet ways in his youth and sowed a few "wild oats." He now was a straight-as-an-arrow rocket engineer complete with a suit and tie. He expected his children to walk the straight line, but this proved to be a difficult task. He seemed to have a selective memory of his own youth when dealing with his sons.

Kay was a Christian woman, who relied heavily on prayer. Vincent was also a man of faith after a somewhat turbulent young life. He had lost his father when he was five and seemed to have no direction in life, until he discovered the world of science and space. He went to a good college and landed a good job. The obstacles, which he had faced and overcame, may have been the reason for his sometimes lack of patience with his straying sons.

Reeny was a gifted child from the beginning, a teacher's dream. At home Reeny was strong willed, always clashing with everyone and always wanting to be in charge. Kay found her young son a daily challenge. Reeny did not respond well to discipline. When he was young, he liked school well enough to behave. When he reached twelve, this began to change. Kay was getting computer pictures sent to her house daily of just what Reeny was up to. This awaited her daily as she reached home after a trying day with five-year-olds. Kay was upset and Vince did not take the news any better. They wondered what to do with their offspring.

The school had a different idea for Reeny. There was a program on the planet Ameriland for gifted students. It was a place with hands-on learning and good discipline. Kay and Vince hated to admit not knowing how to deal with Reeny. They had been there for him in every way, but the trouble at school grew worse. Would they really consider such a move?

Reeny passed the Ameriland exam, even getting in the top 1 percent. It was considered a real honor to go to the Ameriland School. The school was for the top students in hopes of a future in space exploration. Vince and Kay had to pray hard about it. Kay had always been at home for her kids. They were everything. How could she send one away? Reeny seemed excited about the school and wanted to go, so with heavy hearts they said they would let him try it for one year. Vince and Kay feared their young son would otherwise fall into future trouble. Reeny would be coming home on the summer break, just like all the other schools on Earth. Kay thought she could manage to live through this if Reeny could find his way. Reeny's future seemed set, or was it?

*   *   *   *

"Reeny," they called him, one of the youngest flight officers since the year 2900. It was the year 3300. Renfro Charles Gallager, young, eyes the color of the sky and hair dashed with blonde wisps kissed by the sun. His younger brother by two years stood at his shoulder as if he were always meant to be there. Maxwell Leon Gallager, the exact opposite of his older brother in just about every way. He was carefree and somewhat careless, with the darkest of eyes, olive skin that looked like he had been in the sun all the time, and wavy dark hair that could be in disarray had it not been cut short. They both stood in silence as they gazed out of the Starship window. They could have been thinking about their destiny or they could have been wondering how they came to be where they were at the moment.

*   *   *   *

Chapter 1

Kay was roused out of her comfortable moment of peace by the sound of the computer phone.

"Hello," she said with a somewhat weary voice. She knew it could not be good news coming over the galactic space line, for that would be news of Reeny. They did not make such expensive calls to tell you how well your child was doing.

"Hello," she said again, clearing her voice.

"Mrs. Gallager, I'm Mr. Stockwell from the Ameriland School. You probably remember meeting me over the space line when we were discussing Reeny's admission."

"Yes, I do remember you. Is there something wrong?" Kay was hoping he would say that there wasn't a problem, but the look on his face told her differently.

"Well, there is nothing that can't be taken care of. We just had some concerns. Reeny is having a hard time on the shuttlecraft that transports the students from the dorms to the main school. The shuttle driver has written him up several times and

I'm afraid if he keeps having trouble, he will have to ride the Public Canal boat to school. This costs money and is not a very efficient way to school. He would have to get up early and walk to the canals. Maybe you and your husband can talk to him and head this off."

Kay was silent for a moment and with a sigh replied, "Yes, Mr. Stockwell we will talk to him right away, but our space calls are the last Tuesday of every month. Can we get a special connection at an earlier time?"

"Yes, as a matter of fact, Reeny's teachers would also like to have a conference call set up. He has been missing assignments. We all know what Reeny is capable of and we wanted to find some solution that would motivate him in the right direction. There is too much trouble to get into otherwise. Reeny's test scores are high and we realize we are dealing with someone who will get bored quickly. I'm sure we can hit on a good program for Reeny. We always like to keep you parents informed and get some feedback." Mr. Stockwell sounded like a very patient and kind man and Kay was glad he was trying to understand Reeny rather then giving up on him.

"A conference call would be a good idea, just let me know. You can leave a message tomorrow. We will make ourselves available. Thank you for being concerned," Kay said.

"Thank you for your cooperation Mrs. Gallager. I will get back to you as soon as possible with a good time. You have a nice day Mrs. Gallager and try not to worry. Good-bye now."

"Yes, Good-bye." Even before the picture faded from the space computer a tear was rolling down Kay's cheek. She knew her young son needed a certain guidance that no one had hit upon yet. Her heart was heavy, as she had hoped Ameriland might be the answer to Reeny's strong will, but now she had her doubts. She always was a woman of prayer, so that is what she did.

The door banged loudly as Max bounded into the house. Max was all arms and legs. As he threw his disc bag from around his shoulder it caught the crystal candy dish, and with a bang it hit the tile.

"Sorry Mom," he said as the glass shattered all over the kitchen.

"Max I have asked you to be more careful when you are in the house. Just try to pay attention to what you're doing."

"All right Mom, but I wanted to ask you if I can go to a party at Sally's house this weekend."

"I don't know. I need to know more details." Kay knew to find out information directly from parents. She had learned from the experiences she had already had with Reeny.

"Mom, you are going to let me go aren't you? Everybody will be there." Max was continuing toward the steps. Kay knew this trick and wasn't going to fall for it.

"We will see. I will call Sally's parents for details and talk to your dad," Kay said firmly. Max liked an answer before it got to Dad, so he was not happy and took the steps two at a time to his room. Kay was prepared to find out all she could on this "party." This new group of friends he was hanging with was pretty wild and not altogether honest with their activities.

Max was following in Reeny's footsteps when it came to school. Max was given the Ameriland test and also passed it this year. Kay had not let Reeny go to Ameriland until he was fifteen, so she was not sure she could give Max up next year. She saw problems with Max coming rapidly through the friends he had chosen, and wondered if he would be better off in Ameriland. She would have to talk more about it to Vince. It was too hard to let go of her children, and tears were a common thing to Kay. Kay knew getting into the space program at their ages was to be envied among other parents and children. Her boys seemed to take their smartness for granted and did not grasp how fortunate they were. She hoped Reeny would straighten up and not throw this opportunity away and she certainly wanted the same for Max.

Chapter 2

"Reeny hurry, we are going to be late for the boat!" yelled Jon from the dorm hallway.

"I'm coming, you sound like a Krito bird," Reeny yelled back.

"This is all your fault we are having to take Pubcan and ride with all the strange east-side city Canots. I also would like to say how thrilling it is to ride with the Talcots from Russo, they are a real treat. They stare too much with their third eye," said Jon as he picked up his disc bag.

"Now Jon, remember we are all God's children, and take care of what you say. I could not let those bullies cheat the little ones out of their coins for the day," replied Reeny as they continued outside toward the canal.

"You should have let the shuttle driver take care of it," said Jon.

"Oh yeah, like he takes care of everything else," Reeny was saying as he saw the boat about to leave the platform. Both boys took off running down the lush grassy knoll and took a giant leap off the platform and right into the lap of an old Talcot lady.

17

Her third eye stared directly into Jon's eyes. He shook himself off and shivered as he got up. When he turned around Reeny was giving him an amused look.

"As I was saying, thank you for the black eye from the shuttle fight and for a wonderful ride for a month on cruise Pubcan, courtesy Mr. Stockwell," Jon said and motioned with a wave of his arms and a bowing gesture toward Reeny.

"You did not have to fight," Reeny said.

"Oh what was I supposed to do, let them beat the life out of you, since that seemed to be what the shuttle driver wanted to happen."

"Yes, Mr. Brooks has not liked me since I pulled him off Dal. He was pulling his arm off. All Dal did wrong was get to the stop late. He is a physically abusive man with a short temper and should not be driving children anywhere. The school always believes the lies he tells. Remember how he stood in front of the shuttle and said if any one tells on him about anything, he would make their life miserable. I could not stand by and do nothing."

"Reeny did you ever stop to think that it would be us that he made miserable? I mean, look around. He got his perfect chance to see you off the shuttle when you threw the first punch. I mean, really, who won?" Jon asked.

"Quit your whining Jon. I believe people get what's coming to them and he will get his."

"Yeah and we got what was coming to us," Jon said as he looked over the blue green waters of the canal.

"Mr. Gallager, late for class again and I might add not an assignment completed from yesterday. I guess you will take the zero again. I don't care how many tests you pass with 100 percent, you will not pass this class without your assignments complete." Mr. Day was speaking, but it might have fallen on deaf ears. Reeny was already thinking about the trip tonight to Obe Mountain. He would be able to see the Starship Arial take off to Zota. Zota was a planet just discovered and full of new possibilities. Life had not been discovered there yet, but the whole planet had not been explored. Reeny's heart was up in the sky not in a stuffy classroom. Reeny, in his youth, could not seem to understand that he must pay his dues like everyone else and stay in school until that day could come.

Reeny was starting to fail his classroom subjects. The teachers at Ameriland were used to dealing with all types of gifted children and they were determined Reeny would make it even if he proved one of the greater challenges. Reeny was one of the brightest students they had come across and they needed to work out a program that would keep him interested in the class work. What to do with Reeny was a common question.

"Well I just hope they don't call home," Reeny was saying to Jon as they were climbing Obe Mountain that evening.

"Reeny, what do you expect to happen to you? I mean, you know we all miss a few assignments, but you have to turn in something. The virtual classes are much more interesting and we will have more virtual classes the older we get. We just have to do the class work first," Jon said.

"I know. I just can't seem to get motivated. I already know that stuff and I'm bored," Reeny said, as he looked heavenward. "You know, if I pass the test for flight school early, I can leave the Ameriland School a whole year sooner."

"Oh Reeny, you would not want to miss your senior year at Ameriland. There are all kinds of neat stuff to do that year," Jon said.

"I don't care about all that," Reeny said.

"You would have to improve your grades to do that anyway," Jon said.

"I can do that. I've been thinking, as long as I know I can get into flight school quicker, I'll start doing better at school," Reeny said decidedly. Jon just shook his head. Jon knew that there would be no talking Reeny out of anything he had decided on.

That night at the Gallagers' house, things were not going well. Vince and Kay had received the awaited conference call from the school. It seemed Reeny was barely going to pass this year. The teachers were concerned about some of the other boys he had chosen to hang out with, and they had a greater concern about rumored activities. Ameriland had a certain plant that grew very well in the climate there called "marijuana." This plant had been long contained on Earth many years ago, but now had made a comeback as a drug of choice on Ameriland. People alive today could only read about the effect the drug problems had on the Earth youth in the 1960's to 2060's. Now it seemed there might be a renewed interest in the old ancient vice. Ameriland youth were at risk now, and some Ameriland teachers had seen signs that it was reaching into the school. Some students had already been caught and punished and some had been sent home to Earth. Earth children seem to be the most curious of the races and therefore needed a tighter rein. When the Gallagers were told of this newly discovered problem, they knew Reeny could possibly be curious enough to try it. The teacher had confirmed the need to watch Reeny even more closely. His behavior was different and he did not seem to care in the least about his future. He had been caught around those that were smoking the weed, but directly nothing could be proved that he was into it.

Meanwhile the arguments at home were reaching fevered pitch. Both parents were frightened beyond words for their children. They did not know how to handle what had come their way and turned on each other. At times the words cut so deep that the wounded heart seemed not able to heal. Nerves were raw with grief. One can live with most anything, but the hurt a child can inflict upon himself can reach a parent's heart as if stuck by a knife.

"My mom always said, 'When a child is young they step on your toes, but when they are older they step on your heart,'" Kay said. They were in bed talking about the boys.

"I just can't figure out what our kids are thinking most of the time," Vince pondered out loud. He was always trying to get a few steps ahead of those boys and he never could. They always had something going on that would cause some grief.

"Well they do have your strong will," Kay said.

"Don't go blaming me for all this."

"I'm not blaming you. It is a good thing to have a strong will. They just have to be guided."

"Do you think we were right in sending Reeny to Ameriland?" Vince asked.

"I've been giving that a lot of thought and prayer. What comes to me is that Reeny has a wonderful mind and is blessed. That is a good place to be. They want to work with him and I think they will be able to. I also think that Max might be better off there too," Kay said.

"You are so anxious to get rid of our sons." Vince turned on his wife.

"I'm not anxious to get rid of our sons. My heart breaks every time I think about it. I love them enough to give them up for something better. The drug problem has reached the public schools here. I think Ameriland can control the problems better. The schools are Christian based and are not afraid to take action when needed."

"Do you call the reports we have been getting on Reeny better?"

"It does not seem good right now. The Ameriland staff is on top of things. I think Reeny will get better. We will be seeing Reeny for the break in a few short weeks. We can talk to him and then decide what to do with both the boys at that time."

"Well we will see. I need some rest now. I have one of my headaches," Vince said and put his head down on the pillow. Kay was familiar with those headaches Vince got. He got them more and more these days, and Kay figured it was the stress that Reeny and Max had caused recently.

Chapter 3

A Krito bird screeched past as Reeny and Jon were leaning out of the lab window.

"I hate Krito birds. They are so ugly with their long necks and ugly green feathers," Jon said as the bird passed with a screech again.

"Yeah, well they are pretty worthless," replied Reeny as he filled up a thin rubber lab glove with water. They were waiting for their next victim to come under the window so they could drop the glove on his head. Both boys had finished the work and had gotten rather bored. Pranks were commonplace for these two, harmless enough, but usually landed them in school suspension. About the time the next prey was under the window, they were suddenly jerked back. They stared at the scary face of Uno, the school custodian. Uno was from Russo and all of seven feet tall, and when he stared down at them with all three eyes, it was a menacing thing.

"Oh Uno it is only you," Reeny sighed.

"You boys are in enough trouble already and final reports come out soon," Uno roared with his deep voice.

"Oh we were just having fun," said Jon.

"I'll see you have fun while you clean this entire lab and then if you still have time for fun you can start on the bathrooms."

"You can't make us do anything," Reeny protested, knowing at this moment Uno had the upper hand.

All Uno had to do was to look at them hard with the third eye and both boys knew they had better get busy or it would be the office for them. Neither boy could afford to get in any more hot water.

When Uno left the room, he looked back in the doorway and observed the two culprits. He thought about these two often and even sent up a prayer or two for them. They were not like most of the boys at Ameriland. They were high-spirited, and without guidance could fall into the wrong hands. He had seen them with the wrong crowd, but never saw them actually partaking in any wrongdoing. There was a new trend to smoke weed and he thought these two might have tried it, but had wised up quickly enough. Uno knew the teachers here tried to keep a close watch on all the students and he knew also even the best efforts failed. He had seen those that were getting into the drugs and hiding it really well. Outwardly, they appeared to do what they were supposed to do, but behind closed doors, they were heavily into the darker side of things. Reeny pulled no punches and marched to no drum but his own, which may have been why the teachers zeroed in on him. Reeny needed to conform somewhat, after all that is part of life. Uno believed Reeny would do special things in the future, if he stayed away from trouble.

Chapter 4

"I need to get across the canal to see Karu tonight," Reeny was saying as he was observing the red ducks gliding past in the canal. Across the thin part of the canal lay his heart, or so he thought. Reeny had fallen in love with an Amerilander. At fifteen, Reeny felt like any teenage boy with that first big crush. Reeny had always liked the girls; in fact he never went through the stage of hating them. This was different, this felt like the real thing.

Reeny had become even more reckless and headstrong when it came to Karu. Karu went to the all-girls' school across the canal. It was mostly for Amerilanders, but some girls were from Russo and Earth. This was a school well known in the galaxy as the best education for girls.

Karu was already a beauty at fourteen. She had long curly red hair and eyes the color of green emeralds. She was slight in build, but could hold her own. Her coloring was unique for most Amerilanders. They were known for their dark hair and light skin. Karu had a more olive-toned skin. Her hair and eyes stood out even more.

"Reeny you have to give her up, her parents will have you hung," Jon said.

"Don't be so ancient, those laws were done away with years ago. Jon, what is your problem?" Reeny asked.

"My problem is that we are leaving for the summer break and I don't feel like spending time in the detention house. It could cause us to miss the ship home."

"Well go back to the dorm, I can do this without you."

"Sure you can! Who will distract the Boat Security Force while you get one of the paddle boats across?" Jon's voice was getting louder and Reeny put his finger up to his mouth to shush him.

"If you are going to help, now would be the time," whispered Reeny. As if on cue, Jon started rolling down the hill gasping in pain. The patrolmen now were looking at Jon, while Reeny slipped around some bushes to untie one of the paddleboats. The suns were going down and it was not easy to spot the shadowy figure as it crossed the canal to the other side.

"What is wrong with you?" one of the patrolmen was asking Jon as he was reaching out to Jon with all of his twelve fingers.

"Oh, I think I might have twisted my ankle when I fell. It hurts, but I think I'm going to be all right now, thanks," Jon was saying as he was backing away.

"Say, aren't you one of the Ameriland students from Earth?" the tall patrolman asked Jon.

"Yeah, uh I mean, Yes Sir." Jon was becoming more uncomfortable.

"What are you doing out here so late, isn't it near curfew?" The two patrolmen were getting closer.

"I guess it is getting late. Thank you for reminding me. I'll just scamper right back now and you guys have a great evening," Jon was saying as he walked away backward. He turned and took off before the patrolmen could say another word.

Reeny had made it across the canal with no trouble and he knew Jon could talk his way out of anything, so he gave it no more thought. He went up a short hill and was in tall cane that tore at his clothes. It never gets real dark on Ameriland, but in this woodsy grown up area, it was dark. He began to crawl forward and was startled by something that moved near him. With a swish of the bush around him came a creature with glowing eyes. Reeny gasped with fear. He moved a little and a high-pitched squeal came from the creature. He realized he had stepped on the tail of a Sequata.

Sequatas are like Earth's cats. They have shorter tails and bigger rounded ears, more like mouse ears. They have long fur and are many different colors.

The Sequata Reeny just stepped on must have been dark, because he never got a good look at it. He did recognize the sound they make, because it was an eerie sound. He shook himself as he trudged up the small pathway leading to the girls' dorm. He could see the lights on, but he was looking only for one window light because that was where his heart was.

"Reeny this and Reeny that." Scout was prancing around the room with a Krito feather, taunting poor Karu and almost bringing her to tears. She did not want to be reminded of Reeny. It was painful enough that he was leaving in a few days and she had been forbidden to see him.

Scout was from Earth and was Karu's best friend. They had roomed together now for two years. Scout's parents were well off to be able to afford this school, but Scout never acted like a snob. She was friendly, outgoing and popular among the girls. She did tease a lot and this would get her into trouble sometimes.

"Karu stop feeling sorry for yourself, he is just an Earth boy. Why don't you make the trip home with me for break and...what was that noise outside?" Scout asked lowering her voice and turning out the light. She looked out the window. Turning from the window, she put her finger to her mouth. Karu crept closer to Scout and peered over her shoulder out the window.

"It looks like someone is under our window. Oh, what was that?" asked Scout with fear in her voice. A small pebble hit the window again. A smile came across Karu's face and Scout looked at her puzzled at first, but with wide eyes, she realized what Karu was excited about.

"Oh no, Karu don't you go down, you know it will be trouble. Your parents have found out about you seeing an Earth boy. They don't know Reeny, but this could get you both in a lot of trouble if you are caught together. They have threatened to send you to school on the other side of the planet," Scout said in a stern voice.

"Scout, I have to go down, cover for me when they do late check. Will you?" Scout could hardly turn Karu down when she had that big-eyed look and the pouting mouth to go along with it. Before anything else could be said, Karu was out the door and down the steps leaving Scout with her mouth open.

Getting outside the back way wasn't easy, but Karu could count on old Mrs. West to be sleeping soundly. She slipped out the door and hunched over in order not to be seen out of any lower windows. She was looking back to make sure she was safe and smacked into Reeny. They both giggled as they ran toward the canal holding hands.

"Wow, how did you get here?" asked Karu almost out of breath from laughing and running.

"The same way, it is pretty easy to get here, but sneaking back is a problem. I just had to see you again before I left for Earth. When we met at the dance, I never dreamed there would be a problem with us seeing each other. I mean, they gave a dance for the schools to get to know each other, then they get mad if we are attracted to each other. We have girls at our school too, but they are in a different building. Don't they want all of us to date and have a good time? I don't get it."

"Well not all parents feel the same way as mine. My parents would have let you visit if you were not an Earthling. They say it causes too much heartache and trouble."

"It's not like we want to get serious, we are too young for that."

"I know, but when my parents found out that an Earth boy was visiting me, they got real emotional and upset. I don't know how to handle this," Karu said near tears.

"Sorry it has turned out like this. I just like being with you and I think you like being with me." Reeny was as serious as he had ever been and seemed older than his years that night.

"Oh, I like being with you and I want to always be friends, but I don't know how that would be possible. We are worlds apart." With that said, Karu had an amused look on her face.

"Yes," Reeny said laughing. "We are worlds apart."

Both Reeny and Karu said their good-byes with heavy hearts that night. They managed to sneak back to their own rooms without too much trouble. They both thought they could not be any sadder. Each lay awake thinking into the night feeling like the star-crossed teenagers in Romeo and Juliet.

Chapter 5

"Hey Reeny wake up, we have to get on the Pubcan today remember?" Jon was shaking Reeny hard.

"I'm getting up, stop yelling! It is your fault we are riding on cruise Pubcan this time. Let me see, what was it you said to Mr. Brooks?" Reeny was asking as he made his way to the bathroom. Jon had rolled up a wet towel on his way past Reeny and gave him a pop with it, ignoring his question.

Jon was making kissing sounds as they headed toward the canal, hoping of course to tease Reeny further about Karu. It did not work, because Reeny wasn't worried about what anyone thought about his feelings for Karu.

"You know, I had to make up a story when ole sharp nose came by at check the other night," Jon said in a bragging manner.

"So, you are good at making things up," Reeny said as they stepped into the boat and elbowed their way to the other side. It seemed more crowded than usual for some reason and

Reeny felt like he could not breathe. He had no patience for the Russos today and he wanted Jon to stop rattling on. He just wanted to be left alone.

They soon reached the school stop and started to get off when they noticed some of their fellow schoolmates standing around.

"I wonder what they are up to? Hanging around the pier isn't what they normally do," observed Jon. Just then the group of boys spotted the pair coming toward them and starting gesturing them over. They were huddled together as if forming the next move in a football game.

"What's up?" Reeny asked.

"Well we got a hold of some good stuff here to smoke and we were going to try it out. What do you say, are you in?" Peter was excited and a little nervous as he was explaining to Reeny and Jon.

"We are not in. Remember we tried that stuff and don't want anymore. Let's go Jon." Reeny started in the direction of the school, but found his way blocked by the Canal Patrol.

"All right boys, all of you freeze. Well what do we have here? It looks to me like we have ourselves some fellows in a whole lot of trouble with the school as well as the law. Get out the handcuffs, we are taking them in."

With that the four patrolmen began to handcuff the boys.

"Hey wait just a minute, we just got off the boat and were headed to school," exclaimed Jon.

"Yeah, well you made a wrong turn," bellowed one of the patrolmen with a husky voice.

"You will get a fair hearing. If you are innocent your record will be cleared. Let's go, all of you," said another patrolman.

They were guided to the station near the school. This station took care of the school and all the trouble that might occur with the students. Reeny was wondering at this time why he could not seem to steer clear of trouble. If he didn't find it, it found him. Trouble found him big time now. Why did he ever strike up a friendship with those boys? He had found them interesting at first and he liked interesting people. Peter was from Earth and he was smart and athletic. Omar was from Russo. He was not a Talcot, so he did not have three eyes. Omar was good at his studies. Al was an Amerilander complete with all twelve toes and fingers, and he was the clown of the bunch. Moro was from Ameriland too and he was the quiet one, but he could come up with some good ideas for pranks. So here they all were. This is where their carelessness had got them.

Vince and Kay had just settled in for the evening when a space call came in from Ameriland. They looked at one another wearily. "Just two weeks left. I wonder what could be going on?" Vince was wondering out loud as he reached the screen of the computer phone. Kay was looking a little worried as the two answered the phone by pressing the visual button.

"Mr. and Mrs. Gallager, I'm Officer Dell from the school patrol station...uh we have a situation that might require you both to come to Ameriland. We have Reeny here on some drug charges. He says he is innocent and he will get a hearing at the school. Since it was on school property and they are underage, this can be handled through the school. None of the boys should get into too much trouble over this. This is their first offence and we like to give them a chance. I would like to stress that any further activities in this area would put them in serious trouble. It could ruin their future here at this school. We need to get them on the right track. I think they are good kids, but we can't let them go unpunished." With that Kay had gasped and was sitting down holding the sides of the chair. Vince stood still for a moment to take in what he had just heard.

"Officer, it will take us four weeks to get to Ameriland on Space Air. That is if we leave right away, and Reeny is due to start home in two weeks." Vince was concerned about what all this would mean.

"I'm in the process of checking the new law. Since the drug problem has been new here, we have a lot of different laws coming down fast. I believe the law states that if the student is caught actually partaking of the drug, then parents are required to come to a hearing here on Ameriland. I don't think Reeny and his friend Jon had anything on them or were seen with anything. I am not going to have you all make arrangements to come here until I can get to the bottom of this. I will get back with you as soon as I can," Officer Dell said.

"We will do whatever we need to do Officer Dell," Kay said.

"All right then, don't worry too much. We are trying to get these kids to understand the serious effects of drugs and we need to crack down heavily right now or it will be out of control. If Reeny did not participate then he will be coming home. I hope this will scare them out of any further dealings with illegal drugs, even for those just hanging around.

Well I will let you two go... I hope I can get back to you with better news," Officer Dell said with a kind understanding. He had kids of his own and they were not angels, so he always tried to help the parents through these difficult times.

"Officer, thank you for your help. We appreciate any way that would help Reeny at this time. We would like to let him come home if that would be possible. Please let us know as soon as you find out, no matter what time it would be here." Kay was speaking and trying to maintain a calm voice.

"Oh, I will let you know. Maybe when you get to speak to your son, you will feel better. Don't worry about him now. He is safe here at the station. He is scared, but he should be. Try and keep the faith. Good-bye."

"Yes Officer, we will, and again thank-you," Vince said and pushed the button to close.

Both Kay and Vince stood and looked at each other.

"Well he has done about everything now. What else will he do before he gets to be an adult?" asked Vince exasperated.

"I don't know, but I'm tired and I don't even want to talk about it," Kay was saying as she was headed to bed. She had almost become immune to her boys' many adventures and longed for just a normal life.

"Kay now, we have to talk about this." Vince caught her sleeve as she went by.

"No, I don't think I will talk about it. If I do talk about it I will end up screaming and yelling. I just want some peace in my life...you know, just some peace! I didn't ask for perfect children, always doing what they are supposed to, but I just want a normal life."

"I know, but you know it will be alright. We have a lot to be thankful for and our boys are not bad kids, they just get themselves into things. They get bored or something. Look, maybe we shouldn't jump to conclusions. Reeny will have something to say on his side of the story. We need to maintain until then and pray hard," Vince said in a calm manner and he pressed his face to Kay's cheek.

Kay went to bed but could not rest. She had had a hard day at school and was exhausted, but her mind would not rest. She was glad it was the weekend so she could pull herself together before Monday.

A space call came in early the next morning, waking Kay after a rough night. Vince was up and got to the computer phone first. Juggling coffee in one hand, he pressed the button.

"Yes, hello." Vince was nervous, because it seemed too early for a call with news of Reeny.

"Hello Mr. Gallager." Vince could see it was Officer Dell on the screen, and Kay had come around the corner sleepily. The look they gave to each other for that split second was "what now?"

"Oh and hello to you Mrs. Gallager, hope it is not too early, but I thought you needed some good news." Officer Dell seemed way too happy, Kay thought.

"Yes, we could use some good news," Vince said.

"We decided to hold a meeting with the school council last night. We wanted to clear up some things before we brought parents here from other worlds. The cost and time are enormous and it is nearing the end of the school year. We did re-check the new law and it does say if the student has drugs on him, or is using them, parents must appear in person. Now in Reeny's case, the other boys have stated that Jon and Reeny were getting off the canal boat and stopped to talk. The other boys were honest and said Jon and Reeny were headed to school and were not participating in their activities. I think a short hearing on Monday will clear things up for Reeny and Jon," said Officer Dell.

"That is good news. We spent a restless night over this and appreciate your quick call. That says a lot for the other boys involved. It was mature of them to tell the truth," Vince was saying and Kay was agreeing.

"These are good kids from good homes. We were impressed with their honesty when we brought them in. I think they learned their lessons in more ways than one. They were all sick last night. It seems they got a hold of some bad stuff. They tossed their cookies all night. I felt bad for them, but this might have saved their lives. They were pretty scared. The other parents are going to have to travel here, and the boys won't be going home for break due to the timing. Some parents might choose to withdraw their children, but we will see."

"Yes, it is unfortunate for the other parents. This could change these boys' lives one way or the other," Vince said, knowing he could have been in the same boat.

"Yes we feel bad, but if they were not caught now, it could have resulted in a much worse situation down the road," Officer Dell replied.

"Oh, I agree!" Vince said quickly.

"OK, I will let you folks go and you can expect a call from Reeny at his regular time. If all goes as it should, he will be home for break in a matter of weeks. Take care and good-bye."

"Thank you again Officer Dell and good-bye." Vince pushed the close button.

"Now see, we did not have to wait long for this crisis to end. We have an answer to prayer. We can be thankful for the way this turned out," Vince said.

"Yes, sometimes I underestimate the power of prayer. I worry so about our boys, and when it looks so bleak I get discouraged," Kay said.

"Why don't we get some more rest before the other two get up and turn on everything in the house," Vince said.

"Sounds good to me," said Kay crawling back into bed.

Monday morning could not have come quickly enough for Reeny and Jon. Friday night was bad. They, true to form, had argued and worried the night away. Both boys were shaken by this experience and vowed to somehow make changes. They were allowed back at the dorm on Saturday night and were up early Sunday morning for church. The boys took the sermon on Sunday much more to heart than they had previously, and prayed more then ever. Reeny was thinking of his mom and dad. They must be really upset with him. He did not relish the thought of having to talk about what happened. With all the antics he had pulled lately, he would not blame them if they did not fully believe him. Jon looked a little pale sitting next to him in the pew. They had decided to go down to the field after service and play some ball. The Kaltos roamed the field and they had to be careful of them. The adult female Kaltos were the ones to watch out for. They usually saw people as a threat to their eggs. If the boys felt bored they hopped on the backs of the smaller ones and had races. This could be a dangerous thing to do because sometimes Kaltos tried to bite. The thought of playing a little ball and watching the bright green monsters sleuth across the grassy field had put their minds at rest for a while.

Monday the boys were looking across the table at the five adults who were going to decide their future at Ameriland. The boys had not been told that they were going to get off with a warning. The team of adults here felt these boys needed to be on the hot seat for a while, hoping that they would think twice about hanging out where they didn't belong. Of course, they had believed the other boys when they said Reeny and Jon were innocent, but these two had pulled some capers before and lived just on the edge of trouble. They were hoping to stop them from one day, crossing over.

"Well boys, we have been led to believe you two to be innocent of the charges," said Mr. Ray. "What do you have to say?"

"Mr. Ray, we were just walking past the other boys, but we did stop to see what they were doing after they called us over," explained Reeny.

"When you saw what they were doing, what did you do?" Mrs. Win asked.

"We were going to leave, but that is when the patrol officers arrived," Jon replied.

"That seems consistent with the other statements, and one of the officers did say he saw the two just get off the boat. Next time, be more careful when you see suspicious behavior. You two cannot afford to get into any more trouble. Stay clean until time for break and you will go home. Your parents will be given a report of this meeting and you can make your phone calls home this week," Mr. Stockwell said.

"Uh, thank you, we will stay out of trouble. Yes we will stay out of trouble." Both boys were trying to get the words out. They looked at each other with relief.

"You may go to class. Consider yourself blessed that the other boys decided to help you two out and not try to get you in trouble,"

Mrs. Win was saying when the boys were getting up to leave. The two left with hurried good-byes and thankful hearts. They bounced happily down the hall, for the first time, to class.

"Wow, I can't believe we got out of that one. Can you believe the other guys vouched for us? They are not so bad after all," Reeny said.

"Yeah I wonder why. They could have been mean and we would have gone down with them," Jon said.

"I think they may have felt bad enough as it was. I heard they were really sick that night. It was bad stuff," Reeny said as a big girl side-swiped him in the hall. He got his balance back as Jon was asking how he had come to that information, because they had been separated from those boys that night and put into different cells. Reeny explained that he had seen Moro's girlfriend in the hall earlier while he was waiting for Jon to get to the meeting. She had filled him in on what had happened to the other boys that night.

"I think they are going to have to stay here for break, because the parents are going to have to come here for a special hearing." Reeny continued on with the story and the fate that awaited the other boys.

"Ouch, that bites!" Jon exclaimed.

Reeny and Jon talked of plans to go down to the field and race Kaltos after school that day to let off some steam. They went on to class, going through groups of kids that were making remarks about their adventure over the weekend. Some of them were asking questions about all that had happened, but the bell rang and they all had to get to class.

Chapter 6

The trip home was always an adventure in itself. Space travel had become very modern; and with the discovery of black holes and the technical knowledge of folding space, traveling to other worlds was cut from years to just a matter of weeks. It took four weeks to get to Earth from Ameriland. The kids going back home to Russo had a short trip of only two weeks. To the boys of Reeny's age, four weeks was a lifetime, but they were excited as they started the packing. Their summer vacation lasted eight weeks at home before they had to start back to Ameriland.

"Hey Gallager, I hear your little brother will be making the trip back with you. Boy we can give him a hard time," said Will as he poked his head in the dorm room of Reeny and Jon.

"Yeah, you may want to give him a hard time, but he will most likely give you a run for your money. He's worse than his older brother here. The stories I hear from Earth about Max, well it may take all of us to keep him in line," Jon exclaimed.

"Oh we will tame him quick enough," Reeny said.

"I hear 'Ole' Scout's going home on the school spaceship this time instead of the luxury liner her folks usually send for her. I think she may be coming down a little in the world," Will continued.

"Yeah, and I hear you are a little sweet on her," Jon teased.

"She's not so bad looking, but she's a pain in the you-know-what," said Will.

"Oh you don't act like that when she is around. You can't talk hardly, and you start dropping things," Reeny was saying as he observed Will's face turning red.

"You guys should be quiet, at least she talks to me," Will snapped back.

"She likes it when you stammer and stumble after her, she is so spoiled sometimes," Jon said.

"Oh yeah, at least she is from Earth." Will was looking toward Reeny at that point, but before anyone could reply, the night bell rang. They were to get in early tonight, because they had to catch the school spaceship first thing in the morning.

They boarded the spaceship early the next morning and had breakfast aboard. The journey began pretty much unremarkably.

Reeny was still remembering the sight of Karu in the distance waving good-bye. This image would stay with him through the summer break. All the kids were bouncing around him, and he felt as though he were much older than they were at that moment.

Reeny always felt as if he were old beyond his time. He could never quite understand these feelings he had about himself. He always was ready to grow up. Childhood was boring and being a teenager was a drag. He enjoyed a few things that come with being young, but for the most part wished for the day he would be an adult. Now sitting here among his friends he realized that fact even more. He longed for the open space and the possibilities that stretched out before him. He felt he was meant for something else bigger and greater, but felt that he could not share such thoughts with anyone. This is what he kept to himself.

As they eased on into space the beauty was breathtaking, and Reeny took all of it in. The others ragged on him about how quiet he was and they tried to bring him into their game. He was content for a while, Jon left him alone. Jon had been his friend for a long time. They were together at school beginning in the second grade. Jon knew Reeny's moods, and knew when to leave him alone.

He sometimes had the same ways, and probably understood Reeny more than anyone.

At lunchtime, they were all gathered around talking about the things they would do for the next four weeks. There were plenty of things on board to do. They could go down to the virtual reality theatre where they could actually put themselves in a movie part with the characters. The characters were holograms, but, hey, seemed so real it was hard to tell them from the human characters. With the theatre, they could write stories of their own or put themselves in a movie already written. This was a favorite among the students.

Another place they could go was to another virtual reality scene that featured ocean life from Earth. They could actually witness a whole ocean of fun. They were in a room that had a beach and they could go down into the virtual water in a small sub. They could explore anywhere they programmed the sub to go. This was a very good tool for learning the ocean, and an endless amount of fun.

The virtual zoo was another good place. They could pull up any program about animals and be able to be up close to them. They even could take an African Safari.

Ameriland animals were programmed into the system also. The kids could get to know about the animals of both worlds. A new program would be available featuring Russo's animals, by the time they made the trip home. New programs were always being added each trip so the kids would not get bored on such a long trip home.

Of course there was always the gym where they could play the old-fashioned way. A certain amount of time was required in the gym. It was important that they get plenty of exercise, not to say that one didn't get exercise running from a rhino in the virtual safari program, but the students needed real experiences as well. They were encouraged to learn the old ball games and jog on the track.

They could have picnics high on top of a virtual mountain or go to a fancy virtual restaurant. The newest attraction on board was the virtual theme park, complete with roller coasters and other rides that were favorites hundreds of years ago. These old rides proved to be a hit.

The students were all ready to sign up for the various activities that afternoon. Reeny just wanted to stay in his room and look out at the space. That was enough excitement for him that evening. Tomorrow he would explore the different places to go.

Reeny's mind was filled with thoughts of Karu and he welcomed the time alone. Jon had decided to join some other kids and go to the theatre.

Reeny and Jon were sharing a small room with bunk beds. The room was just big enough to stand by the beds with a small table beside them. The closet on the other side of the room was extremely small, so students were discouraged from bringing too much stuff. The small window at the end of the room was the view to open space. If the students wanted better views, they went to the gathering room where there was a spectacular view. There they ate, played small games and talked.

"I just can't get over how small the space is in here. How will I survive this without going crazy?" Scout complained loudly.

"Why did your parents make you come home on the school spaceship, instead of the private ship they normally provide for your transportation home?" Hannah asked.

"Oh it may have something to do with me getting mad on the computer phone with Mom. She doesn't know anything. She says I am disrespectful to her and Dad. They think I am spoiled, and that this will teach me a lesson," Scout replied.

"This isn't so bad. Did you have things to do on the private ship?" Hannah asked as she put away some clothes in the small closet.

"We have a virtual theatre and other small programs. We have thousands of books and games. We have a gym too. You know…" Scout put her finger to her cheek as if in thought and finished her sentence. "This trip could be fun with all the attractions they have on board, and I'll be able to have friends to share the fun with. Hey do you want to go to the virtual beach?" Scout asked with a sudden burst of excitement. Scout was like that. She could make the most of any situation.

"Yes, I think that would be fun. We can go right after we eat," Hannah said. She was glad Scout was feeling better about things. She did not know Scout well and hoped that they would get along. Hannah knew Scout was popular and she felt a little self-conscious around her. She wanted Scout to see her as a friend. She was new this year at school and felt a little out of place. The other girls had been together a couple of years and had established friendships. Hannah had a hard time trying to find her place and had cried herself to sleep many nights, but dared not let the other girls know. She even thought about begging her parents to let her stay home next year and go to a regular school. Her parents were not well off and she was one of a very few girls to receive a full scholarship to the school. Her parents were so proud of her and she did not want to disappoint them. She had feelings of being trapped and scared, and she was looking forward to being at home for a while.

The next day a group had gathered at the virtual beach. Reeny had begun to join in with some of the fun. Karu was always on his mind, but he decided to make the best of the trip and go along with the others to keep busy. Jon enjoyed the beach the best and Reeny suspected it was because this was the favorite hangout for the girls. He figured they would be there a lot. He would really like to check out the virtual ocean later, because his other love was the ocean. He had heard they had put new programs in since their last trip and some of the kids had visited the ocean earlier with good reports on it.

"Hey, look who's coming our way!" Jon punched Reeny's arm, shaking him out of daydreaming. They had been sitting on the beach for a few minutes at that point and had gotten comfortable. When Reeny looked up, he saw Scout waving and walking along the beach. Hannah was behind her. Hannah had pulled her hair back, but her fine blonde hair was slipping out of the knot. Her hair became slightly disarrayed as it blew in the virtual sea air. Jon was immediately captivated by the slight figure behind Scout's darker, more athletic build. The girls stopped to put some towels down on the sand. Sun bathing was a treat for kids and only safe in the virtual sun. There were safety features to keep harmful rays out. Earth people were discouraged years ago from bathing in the sun, due to continuous harmful rays as the decades passed. This particular pastime was now awakened in a new generation. They had found a way to have their beautiful tans without harming their bodies. They had all the joys of the beach and the water without the worry of real dangers.

"I think I'll go speak to Scout," Jon said.

"You never much cared to speak to Scout before," Reeny shot back, clearly seeing through Jon's pretense of wanting to see Scout.

"Well maybe I've decided to be friendly, no use being a snob." Jon was walking away and Reeny shook his head.

"Reeny don't you want to come over with me?" Jon asked and stopped to wait on Reeny. Reeny rolled his eyes and got up. He knew it was no use to try and get out of it.

Maybe he could pick Scout's brain a bit about Karu. He did not want Scout to tease him, so he knew he had to be cool. They greeted the girls when they reached them, and the girls greeted them back. They invited the boys to sit with them and Jon promptly sat down right next to Hannah. Reeny slumped down.

"Jon, this is Hannah Farmer, Hannah this is Jon Lee." Scout was introducing the pair, but Jon was at a loss for words and stammered a "hello." Amused, Scout thought she could have some fun with these two. Hannah was terribly shy too. After she managed to say a "hello" to Jon, she waved to Reeny. Reeny had already met Hannah when he was on one of his incognito trips across the canal to see Karu. He actually had run into her, knocking her down, when he was trying to run from the patrol on the other side of the canal. She was in the park feeding the red ducks when he came tearing through the bushes to hide, and they collided. She knew who he was, because the girls talked about this romance quite often. Reeny was a gentleman and made sure she was fine, introduced himself and asked her to hide him from the patrol. She did a good job of hiding him and has had a secret crush on him since. The blush across her face did not go unnoticed by Scout; but nothing got past

Scout. She would certainly have to get to the bottom of this later.   They made small talk and played in the water until the virtual sunset ended the program.   They needed to get back to their rooms, but before they left, they had made plans to go in an ocean sub program the next day.

On the way back to the room Scout could not resist asking Hannah about how she knew Reeny.   When Hannah explained the episode to Scout, she was laughing very loudly as they entered the girls' quarters.   This caused Mrs. Watts, the hall guardian, to look out of her room to see what the noise was. The girls gave Mrs. Watts a friendly "hello" and passed without making another sound. When Scout reached their room, she threw herself on the bed and laughed.

"I can just picture Reeny now, sitting behind the bushes while you chatted with the patrolman.   Boy do you have something on him," Scout said catching her breath.

"I don't want him to feel uncomfortable around me because of that.   I think it is so romantic, you know like the old ancient story we read in school, Romeo and Juliet," Hannah was dreamily saying.

"Oh pooh, he is just a silly boy and Karu is just as silly."   Leave it to Scout to ruin the mood.

"Don't you think it is romantic for Reeny to risk all to see his love?" Hannah still wanted to make it a wonderful adventure.

"Well I wouldn't risk getting kicked out of school over a boy," Scout snapped back.

"Maybe you haven't been in love," Hannah said.

"Maybe you haven't either." Scout was getting testy and Hannah decided to drop the subject. Hannah was thinking Scout was a little jealous of Karu.

"It will be fun to go to the ocean sub tomorrow, but I'm afraid after that I'm going to have to save my attraction tokens and do more of the free stuff," Hannah said. Scout sat up on the bed to look at Hannah.

"Didn't your parents purchase more tokens? The tokens that come with the trip hardly last four weeks," Scout was asking with concern in her voice.

"My parents did not feel I needed more tokens than they provide for the trip," Hannah said, not convincing Scout. Hannah did not want to tell Scout that her parents were not well off and could not afford any extras. With the scholarship, everything needed was provided, including the regular trips home. Hannah had to live meagerly and did not have the use of any extra frills. She was fine with this herself, but did not like the other girls to know. She was getting good at making up reasons why she did not participate in all the activities at school. Some of the girls had guessed Hannah's predicament and would give her their share of things sometimes. They learned to do it in a way as not to embarrass her. Scout caught on fast to Hannah's plight, and felt bad that she had said anything.

"Oh look!" exclaimed Scout as she was looking through one of her many bags.

"I thought I had lost these tokens. My parents bought me more when I told them I had lost these. Well now I have too many. I don't need all of these tokens. I will just put them away and lose them again. Hey, why don't you take them? They will just get lost or go to waste otherwise." Scout could sound pretty convincing when she wanted to.

"Goodness, I don't think I could take those, they are worth so much." Hannah did not know what to make of this perfect timing, but Scout seemed to have an over-abundance of tokens. She could be telling the truth, knowing Scout didn't worry about money and what went with it.

"Yes you can and you will. I just can't use them all and we might as well have fun together." Scout was persistent and Hannah gave in, thankful for such a good blessing to fall her way. Now she could go to all the attractions like she had always wanted to.

That evening Scout went to the space computer without Hannah's knowledge and asked her parents to approve the purchase of more tokens. She was truthful about what she had done with the other tokens and her parents were pleased that she wanted to help her friend. They approved the purchase and no one else on board knew what a good thing Scout had done for her new friend.

They were able to have a good time together, frequently teaming up with Reeny and Jon on their visits to virtual places. They found the amusement park to be one of the favorite places to go and spent a lot of time there. Not all of the time could be used in the virtual sites. All the kids on board were encouraged to spend quiet time in the library for reading. Some assignments were given to complete on board for school. It was not a lot, but Reeny always had trouble with sitting down and doing his studies.

Reeny got to know Scout really well and he sometimes would talk to her about Karu. He found out many things about the customs of Ameriland families. Some were more rigid then others, and Karu's family was steeped in tradition. This did not make Reeny feel better about the possibility of getting to see Karu on a social basis. He was able to send messages through Scout on the computer space phone. Anything directly coming from Reeny would have been caught by her parents and caused Karu trouble at home.

The trip came to a close quickly and they could detect the small marble they called home in the distant space. They had had a good trip, but were ready to get home and see their families. Seeing them once a week on the space computer didn't mean as much as being able to finally get a hug from their parents, even though no one would admit such a thing at that age.

They still had a day before landing, so they all went to do activities. Reeny, Jon, Scout and Hannah chose to go to the ocean sub. The program began and they were surrounded by ocean life. A shark caught the side of the sub and Hannah jumped.

"This is so incredibly real!" Scout gasped. "I could come here everyday and still be amazed."

"Yes this program is so extensive, you see something different every time you come. It's almost as good as the real thing," Reeny said.

"I took a real Earth voyage in the sea, and you actually see more things in these programs. Some of the real ocean animals were almost extinct from years of pollution. They are making a comeback, but some species are having a harder time. When you go on a real ocean tour, you may not see anything for hours. That is why these programs are so good," Jon added as he was examining a swarm of jellyfish.

The sub continued to submerge deeper into blacker water. The deeper the program took them the stranger the creatures became. The colors of some of these exotic aquatic beasts were brilliantly lit up by the passing sub's lights. The passengers were experiencing a slight chill in the atmosphere due to the program's realistic nature. Hannah was shaking a little and Jon noticed her discomfort and took off the small-weight jacket he wore all the time and put it around her shoulders. Hannah knew the sacrifice Jon just made because these particular jackets were the fashion statements for the teen boys at that time. Almost all boys had this type of jacket on when they were not required to wear uniforms. They were somewhat expensive and really served no purpose. The atmosphere of Ameriland required no jackets most of the time and the ship they were in remained a comfortable temperature all the time, but teenagers of every generation had to have their own look.

Hannah looked down at the blue and white sporty jacket and back at Jon. Jon's face became a little red and he looked away. Jon wished he knew how to act around girls like Reeny did. Reeny seemed to know what to say all the time.

The program was about to end and they had a few more hours until landing. They were quiet as they went into their own thoughts and watched the wonders of the sea. They could have been thinking of how they would spend their summer. When the program ended they went quietly to their quarters to finish packing for home.

Chapter 7

Back at the Gallager home, there were problems brewing with young Max. Max was always finding new excitement where he did not belong. Even though Max had a personality that charmed everyone and was extremely funny, he still was strong-willed and wanted to do things his own way. His way could be trouble sometimes.

Fresh coffee smells filled the air as Vince and Kay stood in the kitchen. They were notified that the school ship would be landing the next day. They were looking forward to seeing Reeny. The last time they spoke to him, he seemed more calm and serious about the future. They had hope that he might be making a turnaround.

"Maybe Ameriland will be good for Max, but the verdict is still out on this whole Ameriland project we've embarked on. I know that a very few kids get this chance for an education and it is Christian based with the best morals in the Universe, but I still am not convinced it is the best thing for our boys. I miss Reeny and now with Max going, I just don't know." Vince was talking to Kay and stopped to sift through some papers that had been faxed that day.

"I know. I feel the same way. The school did not see any other alternative school that would keep Reeny's interest going. I guess I was just scared of his getting into trouble so deep that it would be hard to get out of. We could still consider home schooling by cyber space. For the most part they behave here at home, it is always school that was the problem. I would like to have them home with me," Kay said.

"I don't think that would be a good solution. I think they need to be with others their own age and learn to go along and do what they are supposed to. We can give Ameriland another year and see how the boys do. If we see the need to bring one or both back, we will," Vince said decidedly.

Kay sighed with relief. That seemed a simple solution, after all nothing is permanent. The boys were happy and well adjusted despite her guilt about sending them away. For Kay, motherhood came first in her life since Reeny was born. She was there for every cold and every broken heart. Kay still puzzled over all her sons' needs to pull away and adventure out so early in life. They seemed almost destined for something; and marched toward that goal rapidly. It was something Kay could not understand, but she left them in God's hands, whose hands they were really in.

The Gallagers were on the way to Huntsville from Atlanta to pick up Reeny. There were shuttlecrafts available to take the students home, but the Gallagers wanted to pick up Reeny. Alabama was only a thirty minute hover over. Hovercrafts made it possible to get anywhere faster, long since surpassing the gas hungry vehicles in the early years of travel. Some students came from other parts on Earth and had to take space shuttles home. The Gallagers were thankful that everything was convenient for them.

"It's such a nice day for the ride over," Kay was saying as she looked out the window. She could not wait to see Reeny and she was at peace. Max and Luke were playing games in the back of the craft. The craft was made like the old car vans, but longer to adjust to the hologram game unit in the middle. Small hologram figures appeared from the platform on the unit and different games were played. This was something like the old video games of the past, except the holograms had real images projected out. At home the boys used the playroom with the life-sized images to interact with.

"Yeah, it is a nice day for a hover ride. It will be good to see Reeny and have him home a while. I wonder how Jon will be getting home. Since his parents moved to Texas, we haven't heard from them much," Vince said.

"His mother called the other day. I told you about that!" Kay said.

"No you did not!" Vince snapped back.

"Yes I did. I remember the whole conversation. We were on our virtual walk in the playroom. Remember, we decided to program a walk in the mountains. It was the new program we bought." Kay was getting frustrated because this happened a lot. Vince forgot conversations between them frequently. She always felt so unimportant at these times.

"You didn't say a word about Joyce calling. I would have remembered." Vince was getting firm with his voice and this made Kay bristle.

"I can remember everything that was said that day, but you, on the other hand, can not remember what I said a minute ago. You want to know why? Because you think I'm not as intelligent as you are. I'm no rocket scientist like you are, but I know I'm smarter than you on some subjects." Kay was in the attack mode and probably nothing was going to calm her down until she was proven right.

Vince sat quietly looking out the window trying to think what his next move would be. Should he pretend he had heard this conversation about Joyce, or should he plead guilty? Oh anything could go wrong for him right now. He knew his mind wondered during some of their walks as Kay chattered away about things. He tried to tune in on the important stuff. He was in trouble for sure and did not want the argument to get heated.

"Hey Mom and Dad, we are hungry." Luke was scrambling up to the front and Vince saw this as a chance to get out of hot water.

"What do you say to stopping a while and having some food Kay?" She had that look like "this isn't over," but agreed to stop.

Kay looked at Vince's silly grin and knew she would forgive him again, but she wasn't letting him off the hook so easily. They had been married long enough to know what buttons to push and when to back off.

While they ate, Kay decided to remind Vincent of the conversation she had had with Joyce. She did not want to argue at that time, so she retold the story. Jon's parents had decided to go over and pick him up. Kay said she hoped to be able to get with them and spend some time together before they started back home. Vince agreed with Kay. Kay could not help rolling her eyes, knowing all this had been discussed before. She went along with what Vince said as if it had never been said before. Sometimes one just had to be diplomatic and Kay was getting pretty good at that. She knew Vince had a lot on his mind these days with the new contract starting up at work. They left the small fast food place and they had fifteen minutes left to go. The brothers were getting excited about seeing Reeny, and they were bouncing in the back.

"Settle down you two!" Vince shouted toward the back of the craft. Max was almost fourteen and Luke was almost nine, both were happy and played hard. Sometimes the rough playing resulted in injury despite Kay's repeated warning. When they were together the noise and the playing got intense. Summers were always hard on Kay, because the boys were always into something and they had tons of friends over. Kay loved to have them home, even though she knew the summer wasn't going to be a peaceful one. She hoped she could find plenty for them to do.

They entered the gates of the Space Station and Kay craned her neck to see if the ship had come in. Kay was secretly hoping that they were early enough to see the landing, something that still fascinated her.

"Look Mom and Dad!" Luke was looking at the sky and pointing. They all looked in the direction Luke was indicating and realized the space ship was coming in for a landing. Kay was excited and wanted to leave the confines of the van as quickly as possible. Vince found a place to park, and they all jumped out of the craft like rats off a sinking ship. They ran to the open area to see the spectacular sight. The sky was beautiful as it opened up and the ship came floating in as if on angels' wings. Kay was clapping her hands and did not realize it. Vince noticed Kay's excitement and he hurt for her, because he knew what sacrifices Kay had made this past year. Only a few short weeks and Max would be gone and Kay would have to handle that as well. Kay's biggest job was motherhood and she wanted to make the best decisions for her kids. Looking into her face at that moment would sum up the inner turmoil she was going through, and Vince loved her even more.

They watched the steady stream of kids getting out of the ship, but were watching with eyes only for the towheaded child of theirs. Reeny, now turning sixteen soon, had grown up and filled out since the last time they saw him, and almost walked past them.

"There he is!" shouted Luke. By the time everyone looked around, Reeny was almost past.

"Hey, Reeny, you bone head!" Max shouted, teasing as always. Reeny did not need to turn around to know who had just taunted him. He quickly turned and ran over and grabbed Max around the neck and roughed up his hair. The two got into a tussle. Luke jumped in to join the fun. They were playing like polar bear cubs in the artic sun.

"Well just like old times," Vince said as he went to break up the brothers. As usual they were causing a stir. Before Kay could get to Reeny, he snaked past his dad and straight to her. He gave her a big bear hug and they all had a great group hug. Kay had quickly noticed the physical change in Reeny, and her heart gave a tug. He was growing up and she was missing parts of his life. Reeny saw his mother's face and knew her too well. He gave her one of his winning smiles and the tension was lifted. He wanted her to be happy with her decision to let him go to Ameriland. He truly felt like he should be there even though he had not been a good student. He wanted to work on a few things in his life and he needed to confide in his mom about Karu. He did not know how she would feel, but he knew her to be a fair person.

They had a nice visit with Jon's parents before they parted ways, everyone looking forward to the break each in his own way. The Gallagers' vehicle on the way home was full of life and movement. The brothers constantly picked on each other and Kay was trying to get them to calm down.

"It's no use Kay. Trying to get them to quiet down would be like trying to get the animals at the Zoo to stop making noise," Vince said, noticing Kay's discomfort at how loud the boys were getting.

"Well hearing them together is really good, but usually someone will be yelling before long." Before the words were out of Kay's mouth, a scream came from the back and then crying.

"What is going on?" Vince yelled back.

"Luke is such a baby." Max was headed up to the front and Luke was stumbling after him holding his head and crying.

"What happened?" Kay asked, almost afraid to know.

"Oh, Luke always cheats at virtual racing and then expects us not to do anything about it, he is so spoiled. We hardly touched him, and look how he is acting," Max said looking at Luke.

"Leave the baby up front with Mom and Dad. Max, come back and finish the game," Reeny was saying as he peeked around the partition that separated the back of the van.

"OK, I'll be back. Hey baby, you stay here." Max was talking to Luke, who was trying not to cry with his bottom lip poked out.

"Max, behave and be good to your brother," Vince said.

"Luke, stay up here with us, I have your favorite cookies." Kay wanted to separate the boys at this point, at least for a while. When Luke had finished his cookies and everything was quiet in the back, he fell asleep. When Kay and Vince realized Luke was asleep, they both smiled at each other.

Chapter 8

Summer vacation started with the usual noise and hoopla around the Gallager house. Friends in and out, the noise of the boys was music to Kay's ears at times, but at other times it was trying. Reeny was more independent each year he grew older, and he had a bad habit of staying up too late. Max was hanging with some boys that appeared to be from nice homes, but things did not seem right with him. Luke was up early and played hard, and he loved to explore the creek out back. Kay tried to monitor the boys as best she could and this took up most of her time. She did not resent this for she felt this was what she was supposed to do as a mom. She sometimes felt out of kilter with some of the other moms who seemed to have their own lives and careers, while the children were left to their own devices. I guess you could say she was a bit old-fashioned, but she felt very strongly about being with the children, no matter how old they got.

"Hey Mom." Reeny came from the downstairs play area and was getting into the cold unit. The cold unit was a lot like the old refrigerator except it worked on voice command. The unit delivered the food or liquid to the open panel in the front. Everything came in easy packs, and a screen on the side kept a record of how much was left of certain items. Kay just had to push in the order and the groceries were delivered in a matter of hours. Reeny was busy getting his food out of the front, but was thinking of what to say to his mom. He was concerned with Max's friends. He knew he did not do things the way he was supposed to either and he might seem hypocritical.

"Mom, how do you feel about Max's new friends?" Reeny was a little uncomfortable with this rather adult conversation he was embarking on. He waited for his mom to reply.

"Well I don't know. They seem to be good kids." Kay was wondering what Reeny was getting at.

"Mom, I know this may seem strange coming from me, but I think Max is getting into trouble with these fellows. They are not what they seem. Max might be in over his head with this group of guys and things may be getting out of control." Reeny sounded serious and Kay stopped everything she was doing at the computer to listen.

"Reeny, what do you know?" Kay was getting that strange feeling in the pit of her stomach.

"Mom, they have been sneaking out at night. I don't like being a snitch, but something has to be done. I know I pull pranks and all...I just think this is more than pranks. I think Max goes along with them to save face. They are rich, spoiled and dangerous."

"Well, coming from you, I would say this must be serious. Where do they go at night? They are thirteen and fourteen and can't get around in a hover craft." Kay was trying to comprehend what Max could be up to.

"I don't know, but I think they are vandals and they are into other things... like smoking and uh... maybe drugs."

"Have you seen this behavior in Max?" Kay was getting panicky.

"Not directly," Reeny said.

"OK, thanks for this news. I'll talk to Dad about it." Kay wanted to confront Max right then, but decided to wait for Vince to come home. Reeny finished getting his food and went back downstairs and Kay tried to work on her computer. She couldn't think of anything except Max. She was wondering how he was sneaking out at night. She thought she was a light sleeper and Vince woke up at every little sound. How could her kids get so much past her when she tried to watch them so closely? She knew it would be a while before she got another good night's rest.

Vince came in the door at promptly 5:00. He was hardly ever late and would call if he saw he was going to be late. One thing Kay knew, Vince was as prompt and reliable as the sun rises and sets every day. She loved that part of him, but missed the carefree part of herself she gave up years ago to comply with his rigid ways. He was on time everywhere he went, dressed appropriately always, picked everything apart and turned everything upside down before making any commitments. A true Rocket Engineer. Kay was a bit more flexible, after all, how could you teach Kindergarten and not learn to go with the flow. Sometimes these differences caused arguments, especially when vacation time rolled around. Vince liked to plan way in advance, know exactly what the daily schedule would be and how much money was to be spent. Kay wanted to just pick up and go somewhere and worry about all the pesky things later. Vince sometimes tried to do things the way Kay would like, but when they would get lost on the road, he could not see the fun side of things. Kay would laugh at these things but she knew it was just too difficult for Vince to handle. Why couldn't he just see the humor when she held the virtual hand-held map upside down or when she told him to go West instead of East. She had noticed, however, that with each passing year Vince was becoming less rigid. It could be due to the fact that the children had minds of their own and needed guidance instead of being dictated to. Vince saw he could not control his children like a science project. With the news she was going to give him about Max today, she hoped she would see the milder side he had been working on.

"Hey honey, your husband is home," Vince said as he stuck his head in the door. Kay had made coffee for him because he loved the smell as he came in the door and he drank coffee all day. She was setting the stage for a hard discussion about Max.

One look into Kay's eyes told Vince there was something afoot, and he wanted to just rest peacefully. Kay put a cup of coffee in his hand, greeting him with a smile and kiss. Vince knew he was trapped and he just might as well hear what the boys had done.

"We have meatloaf coming out of the oven soon. I hope you will like it. I ordered up a new kind and it is programmed to come out in thirty minutes," Kay said smiling.

"Yeah, I'm sure I will." Vince did not ask the boys' whereabouts like he usually did. He just wished Kay would come out with whatever it was that was bothering her. She was humming some unknown tune as she was checking the programmed meal monitor. Vince rubbed his eyes. He was getting one of his headaches. He sipped his coffee and she turned around.

"What is it this time?" Vince asked. He could not stand the tension any longer.

"Reeny said Max was sneaking out at night with those boys. I thought I could hear everything at night, but I must sleep sounder then I thought. Oh I am mad! I've been about to explode all day. What could he be thinking? Reeny says they could be smoking and doing drugs. He also said they were probably causing trouble in the neighborhood." Kay blurted this out way faster then she had intended. She had wanted to remain calm. She took a deep breath and looked at Vince. He just stood there with his coffee in midair and stared at Kay.

"Well, I thought those boys were up to no good," Vince said.

"Oh Vince, you always think the boys' friends are up to no good. You never trust any of them and some of them have been good," Kay shot back.

"I just wish that the boys would direct their energy somewhere else. They all could use a little old-fashioned reading. They play too much on those virtual games, and maybe they get too many bad ideas from them," Vince said in the usual tone when the boys were upsetting him.

"Right now, I think we have to figure out Max's problem," Kay said in a softer voice.

"What is the problem? He just has to stop being so lame and easy to be led into trouble. Or maybe I'm wrong, he may be the leader."

"I don't know. Reeny seems to think that he is being bullied into things he knows are wrong. He is afraid to stand up to them. At least that is what Reeny was trying to say."

"We need to talk to Max later. I'm just sure he will confess," Vince said in a sarcastic way.

"He may, if he is scared enough." Kay was concerned and wanting to get to the bottom of this as soon as possible.

They talked to Max that evening, and true to form he became angry with the Gallager temper. He wasn't giving in easily.

They all went to bed with unresolved issues. Kay hoped for a better day the next day. She wasn't going to sleep much that night. She would stay up all night to keep her son safe. Vince could sleep through most anything, and she looked over at him as he snored away. He could escape into the world of sleep, and she envied him.

The next evening the group of boys came by and went straight around the side of the house to the lower level. Max let them in. Vince was looking out of the window and observed the swarm of girls and boys pouring in downstairs.

"What does Max think he is doing, having a party?" Vince asked.

"Call downstairs and ask Max to come up. I think this group needs to go home. They think this is a party house, or something." Kay was looking at the kids still coming in. Vince was walking the floor, trying to decide how to handle this situation the best way possible. They heard loud banging and shouting coming from below and the kids were streaming out of the basement. They were not leaving quietly and Reeny came loping up the stairs with a strange look on his face.

"What happened down there?" Vince asked.

"I think Max told them to get lost, they had beer and stuff. Max knew he would be in trouble as soon as you smelled that. They were mad at Max and stormed out," Reeny said.

"Where do these kids get the idea that they can do stuff like that. Kay you need to call the parents. I never heard of such acting out at their age. Where do they get the beer and other things?" Vince was pacing. Kay rolled her eyes. He was once again putting the hard stuff on her.

"I will call the parents if I can, but they are sneaking it from home probably," Kay said.

"All the more reason to call or hover right over to their houses," Vince said.

"Oh, are you going with me?" Kay asked Vince.

"No, I'm going to talk to Max." Vince left the room and went down the steps.

Kay cyber called as many parents as she knew, but the response was not good. Most did not believe their children were involved with anything like that. Some did not want to be bothered. Kay began to see how these children got to where they were. They had formed a gang to make up for the family togetherness that they craved. They were wealthy, successful families in every way, but it seemed at the expense of these children. What had happened to people? Some of the parents were away on space trips and the children were left with other families or older siblings. Kay wanted to reach out to these kids and her heart was big, just not big enough for this. She prayed for the kids and the parents well into the night. She heard a noise out front, like breaking glass. She heard shouting and went to investigate. She went to Max's room and found it empty. Her heart beat faster as she went to Reeny's room. It was empty too. Luke had spent the night with a friend, so he wasn't at home. She was standing in the hall alone and she felt helpless. Vince came down to check on things.

"You woke up. I didn't think you heard anything," Kay said to Vince as he was looking around. He realized they were alone.

"I guess I'll check outside. What do you suppose they are up to?" Vince asked Kay in an exasperated voice. Kay shook her head. There was no sign of the boys and Kay was getting terrified. When she became frightened, she could feel out of control. She tried to remain calm and cyber beeped the boys, hoping they had their systems on them. She was close to tears when this failed to get results.

"They are not wearing their cyber phones," she said to Vince when he returned inside. She looked out of the window again when she heard noises. She could see two figures approaching the house.

"That's Reeny and Max coming down the street!" Vince said as he walked toward the front door.

They came in with a huff and Max looked white-faced with fear. He was out of control with emotion and Kay was having a hard time understanding him. Vince was following him around trying to get to the reason why his household was thrown into turmoil.

"Reeny, can you explain why your brother is so upset and why you were out at this time of the night? Vince asked.

"Dad, I think we need to call the patrols. They broke the outside light and threw bottles all over in front of the house. There is a bunch of glass out in the street!" Reeny was saying in an urgent voice. None of this was making sense to Kay or Vince. Max was throwing his hands up in the air and walking around the room. He was saying something about it being his fault, and he seemed out of control. He was on the verge of tears. Kay had never seen him like this.

"Son, you need to slow down and explain what is going on here," Vince said, trying to calm the boys.

"Those idiot kids Max was hanging around with paid us another visit and it wasn't for fun and games." Reeny was very mad with Max at this point for letting these kids around the house.

"Max, what happened?" Vince asked.

"They came around the house and knocked on my window. I told them to go away and I was not going to hang with them anymore. They called me an Ameriland snob, and they threatened to get even with me. Mom and Dad, these kids can be dangerous." Max was truly sorry and upset over the whole thing. Vince could not be mad when he saw how frightened his son was. Kay's heart went out to Max.

"Max, why were you outside? If these kids are dangerous, they could have ganged up on you. It was upsetting to go down and see both of your rooms empty and not know what was going on." Kay was still trying to understand the situation.

"I tried to get him to stay in, but he would not listen. He was so mad at their threat. I think he could have took them on. When he went out I followed him, because you know...he could not fight them alone. It's a good thing they were long gone," Reeny was saying, quite pleased with himself. Kay shook her head in disbelief.

"Why didn't you wake me?" Vince asked.

"We knew you had to get up in the morning and go to work. We didn't want to bother you," Reeny said with a sheepish look on his face as he glanced over at the clock. He realized now how silly that sounded with his dad already up trying to sort things out.

They made a report to the neighborhood patrol. Nothing could be done until morning. They all went back to bed.

"Are you asleep?" Vince rolled over in the bed to ask Kay.

"Of course not," Kay replied and turned over to face Vince.

"I think Max learned a very big lesson this night," Vince said.

"I think so too. I think those kids showed their true side to Max and he has had enough of them. It hurt me to see him so upset and disappointed," Kay said.

"Yeah, I couldn't scold him anymore when I realized Max was in such a state of mind. I think he had enough punishment from the real life experience of making a bad choice of friends. If these kids are the popular, good group at school, I would hate to see any of the so-called 'bad kids'," Vince said.

"Yes that is a scary thought. I knew that kids were left to their own devices a lot, but I never dreamed it could get this bad. Where are the adults that they don't know their kids are out prowling all night?" Kay asked, knowing Vince had no answers.

"Ameriland is looking better and better at this time. Right now I'm feeling pretty blessed that the boys are going back together," Vince said.

"Yes, it hurts to see them go. The schools here teach no morals, and the Ameriland School is a rare opportunity for them. I feel the minds God gave them can be put to better use there," Kay said with a tired voice. With that they fell asleep in each other's arms.

Chapter 9

Sunday came around and as usual the Gallagers went to church. Kay's parents were lifelong members there and so Kay got to see them every week. The grandparents looked forward to seeing their grandchildren every week. They were getting older and Kay was glad they lived near enough to see them often. Grandma never really saw much wrong in all of her grandchildren and encouraged them every step of the way. They were so proud that Reeny made it to Ameriland and just as proud now that Max was also going.

Church was an important part of the boys' lives. They had been in many activities there and had learned many valuable lessons. That Sunday, they took their usual seats in the pew. Max had been quiet for a while after the incident with the gang of kids. He was sorry he had caused so much trouble for his parents. He could not express this to his parents of course, because it is hard for teenagers to express themselves. No, Max had to save face and act tough on the outside, while his insides quivered. Reeny did not say much about it either. He looked at it as if he were some sort of a hero, coming to the rescue of his little brother. Luke found out about what happened like he always does. He knew how to be quiet without anyone knowing, while listening to the conversations. That is how the youngest children of families always find out what they want to know.

It did not take long for Max to spot a few friends in the back and head toward them. Kay and Vince looked at each other, because Max was always the "social bug." A few girls in the front were giggling and turning around looking toward Reeny. He was cute and popular, even if he wasn't the social type. They hoped he would come up and sit with them, but when he just nodded at them, they turned around in disappointment. Kay and Vince missed none of this. Luke asked for paper to draw on, just like he always did.

"Why don't you try listening to the sermon once in a while, instead of drawing? Grow up," Reeny said to Luke.

"Why don't you?" Luke retaliated with a shove. This of course caused a shoving match. Vince reached around Kay and caught Reeny's shoulder.

"Reeny, you're one to talk about growing up. Stop that!" Vince could have a stern voice. Kay just rolled her eyes. Why did they cause a commotion wherever they went?

Not much had changed in the Church's design in all the years that had passed. The churches all remained holy looking. Stained glass windows had become popular again. Kay looked around at the pictures in the stained glass and got lost in them. The pulpit was still up high in the front and the choir behind it. You would think you were sitting in the church hundreds of years ago, if you did not see the floating offering plates going down the aisle. The ushers wore hover shoes to get down the aisles faster and help the people get to a seat or answer a question. These things put aside, Kay still liked to pretend she was in the past, thinking about the history of the church and its people. She was roused out of her solitude by the sound of the choir.

The sermon was good and she hoped Max was listening. She did not know if he was paying attention when he was in the back with his friends. Reeny always looked like he was listening, and Luke was doodling away.

Sunday school was fun with the virtual reality theater, where the characters of the bible were holograms. Kay taught a class of fourth graders in Sunday school, and they loved this part of the morning. They did other activities too, but Kay always thought they got more out of the hologram program.

When they got ready to go, they walked out to the parking lot to retrieve the hovercraft. They were walking past some boys when they heard them saying something about Ameriland. They turned around when the group got louder.

"Hey, Ameriland snobs." They could not tell who had spoken and Reeny was making his way to the circle of guys when Vince pulled him back.

"Take this up another time and don't be so feisty. They are trying to get you to respond negatively. Don't give in, be the bigger fellow," Vince said.

Reeny gave them a look and continued to walk with his parents. He got this sometimes now that he was home, and he was tired of it. He would like to take this up another time and place. Vince and Kay wondered what would have happened had they not been around.

One Wednesday evening the house was empty except for Vince. He had a headache, otherwise he too would have been gone. Kay had women's meeting at the church and the boys were off in various directions. Vince's headache had gotten better and he decided to fix a door Max had slammed too hard one time. Max was hard on things sometimes and he always got a lecture about taking better care of things. The tool needed for the repair of the door was not where it was suppose to be. Vince went looking through the house for it and was fussing to himself. He could only guess one of the boys had been in his tools. Most likely Max was the one, since he was the one who always took things apart. When he was little, he would take apart his toys to see how they worked. None of the toys survived the boys' early years. Vince was getting angry at the lack of respect Max had shown for other people's things and here he was trying to fix a door that had been torn up by Max. Shaking his head, he entered into Max's room. He hated to go into the boys' rooms because you never knew where to step. There were clothes on the floor and you couldn't see underneath, which made it treacherous because sharp objects were hidden in the mass on the floor. Walking barefoot or in sock feet could cause serious injury. Vince wondered how the boys could live like this and fussed about it often. Kay's solution was to close the door and go about her business. She actually succeeded in getting that awful image out of the mind, and she didn't dwell on this bad habit of the boys. There were too many other things to worry about. Vince got his nose out of joint every time he had to make a trip to the boys' suite. He tried to avoid it, but today he knew his tool was lurking underneath that sea of destruction and so he went for it.

"Ah, I found you!" Vince said to himself as he lifted up the tool, pulling off the pair of pants attached to it. He got ready to leave when he noticed the window open, and wondered why it would be open in the climate-controlled house. He went over to close the window and forgot to watch his footing when he stepped on some unknown sharp object. With a yelp, he was hopping around. From the corner of his eye, he caught a ray of light coming from beneath the closet door. Curious and wounded he limped over and opened the door. The light seemed to be coming from a clothes hamper that was an antique of Kay's. It was a basket-weave design and the light was shinning through it. There was a flip top and Vince opened it. There was a plant inside with a grow light. He gingerly lifted the potted plant out and realized immediately what it was. A marijuana plant, something he had not seen since college. The drug problem had been under control for many years prior to his youth, but he still remembered a few rebels with the stuff. They were usually considered outcasts among their peers. If you had seen the plant, you never forgot what it looked like or smelled like. Holding the plant and looking around, Vince mused, "Well what else was he going to use his closet for, certainly not clothes."

Kay beat the boys home that evening and was greeted by Vince in the kitchen.

"Hi honey, what's up?" Kay expected the usual greeting and did not notice when she did not get it. She tapped Vince's face with a kiss and went about her business.

"I need to call Luke home from Peter's house. I told him he would have to come home when I got here." Kay was putting some books on her desk. "They were selling books at the church library. I could not resist these books; some of them would be good for my kindergarten class." Kay was always thinking of things that would help her with her kindergarten class, and frequently spent the summer preparing for the fall.

"Kay, don't call little eyes and ears just yet," Vince said.

"Why, are you feeling romantic?" Kay was teasing Vince, but when she saw his face, she knew something was up. Vince stepped away from the counter, where his body had hidden the plant behind him.

"What is this, are you buying me plants now? Vince you know I kill everything. I don't have a green thumb." Kay was examining the plant. Kay remembered seeing something like this, but was trying to wrap her mind around it, when Vince said, "It is a marijuana plant in case you didn't know."

"Yes, that is what this is. I've seen pictures of this before. Vince how come you have one? They are illegal." Kay was still trying to figure this one out.

"Well, maybe someone should have told Max that." Vince told her the story of discovering the plant. Kay was in shock.

"Vince, if the authorities had found this, we could have lost everything. The penalties are high for this!" Kay was in her excited state.

"Look, you don't have to tell me, but Max needs to understand this fact. Where is he anyway?" Vince asked.

"He is at a swim meet in Ben's neighborhood. Do you want me to beep him home?" Kay already knew the answer to that and made her way to the phone.

"It will take him a while to get here on his hover board. Should I beep and say we will pick him up?" Kay asked.

"No, let him come home on his own, I'm still stewing." Kay knew what that meant and left the room.

When Max hovered up on his board, they were in the den trying to busy themselves with something. Vince heard the commotion in the garage. Max always made a loud noise when he arrived home, sometimes singing a made up song.

"There he is. He is too happy. I hope he was at a swim meet and not off doing something else, maybe illegal." Vince was not calm yet.

"Now Vince, you need to get a grip," Kay said.

"Yeah, I'd like to get a grip, right around his little neck."

"Vince, stop it, you know you don't mean that."

"Hey parental units, I'm home. Why did you beep me home, I was getting along with this great girl and... 'beep'... 'beep'...come home now. I mean what is this? Can't a fellow have some fun?" Max was saying in a mocking voice.

Vince brought out the plant from the kitchen and just stood still.

"Maybe you have an explanation for this. Let's see, could this be getting an early start on a botany class for Ameriland?" Vince asked in a sarcastic voice.

"Well uh, no, but it is not mine. It is somebody else's," Max said.

"Um, that's a good answer, but you are the only one who occupies your room. Care to try again?" Vince was trying to hold it together.

"It really isn't mine. I just was keeping it and growing it for him. I wasn't going to do anything else with it, honest."

"Who's him?" Vince asked.

"No. That I won't tell."

"Could this have something to do with the trouble we had with that gang of thugs the other night? Perhaps they wanted this back, or they wanted you to do something else illegal?" Vince asked still trying to get Max to answer.

Max started getting angry as he always did when confronted.

"You won't believe me, you never do. You're always accusing me of something."

"Maybe because you're always doing something," Vince said and Kay shot him a look.

"Well, I don't have to stand here and listen to this!" Max started to walk away.

"Don't you dare walk away son, this is serious stuff. Do you realize that those rowdy kids, in their states of mind, could have called in an anonymous tip to the neighborhood patrol? If they had found this, we could have lost everything. Mom and I didn't work hard and go to school to better ourselves so some punk kids could come around and ruin it for us." Vince was stern and wanted Max to understand what he was saying.

"They would not have done that," Max said.

"Yes they would, if they thought they were not going to get this back," Vince said holding the plant up. "What were you planning to do with it?"

"I was planning to give it back."

"When?" Vince asked.

"I don't know, sometime, just leave me alone." With that said, Max loped down the stairs.

"This could have ruined his chances of going to Ameriland. He has to stop this kind of thing." Vince turned around to talk to Kay.

"I know, but we are blessed you found it." Kay sighed.

"Oh, and what have I not found so far. Should I go check the basement?"

"Vince you are doing it again."

"Yeah but look what my suspicious mind has brought forth. You know...this is really a fine specimen. If he could direct his effort to something legal, he could do just about anything," Vince said, giving the plant a good once-over.

"Vince, get rid of that now. I have to call Luke home," Kay said.

"All right, it is going into the disposal. Every part will be ground up. It is probably worth a lot of money." Vince was acting like he was thinking it over.

"Stop joking Vince, get rid of it now."

"Oh all right." Vince put the plant in the disposal. The grinding noise was heard throughout the house. Kay wondered what Max was thinking at that moment.

"I wonder if those boys will come back after Max?" Kay asked.

"Probably not, but we have to keep a close watch the rest of the summer. I will have to check the boys' rooms more often. Maybe I should look around in Reeny's room. I don't like going down there. It makes me mad to see how messy they are. I know Reeny can't get away with that at school," Vince said.

"Maybe that is why he is so messy here at home."

"You know, Max may have a tougher time adjusting to Ameriland then Reeny did," Vince said.

"That's a scary thought. The cyber space phone line will be smoking by the time he graduates," Kay said.

"It might be burning," Vince said back.

All the boys' birthdays fell in the summer. Kay was glad now for this because they could celebrate with them at home. Luke's birthday had been early summer and they had had a pool party. He was still young enough for that sort of thing. Reeny and Max wanted no part of a party, so they were taken out to the virtual theatre and a nice place to eat. Reeny turned sixteen and could legally drive a hovercraft. This was another reason Kay was glad Reeny would be at school. The only transportation available to the students was the school shuttle or Pubcan. She thought Reeny knew more about the public canal transportation then he wanted to. Max turned fourteen and was sprouting up.

Time was flying by and Kay's heart was getting heavier with each passing sunset. She didn't know how she was going to handle both the boys gone. She tried not to dwell on this as the lazy summer began to wane. Trees were beginning to take on a fall look early, but the heat was still heavy in the South. There had been no more trouble out of the gang of kids and for that Kay was thankful.

The last remaining two weeks of vacation were hectic. Kay was trying to get the boys prepared to take off for Ameriland; and it was harder to get two ready then it had been for one. Clothes were bought and other items were packed ready for the trip. All the family would be at the Station to see them off.

All the cousins, aunts and uncles were proud of the brothers and wanted to be there when they took off. It was still an exciting thing to watch, even with all the space travel. Not everyone had traveled in space. It was still an expensive adventure.

It was interesting at the Space Station. Airplanes flew out at warp speeds carrying people to places on Earth, and space ships took off daily. It took very little time to travel from planet to planet, country to country or just state to state.

Reeny was looking forward to returning to Ameriland and seeing his old buddies, especially Jon. Reeny had meant to tell his parents about Karu, but never felt it was the right time. Max seemed to give them enough to think about. He knew he would have to keep an eye on Max at school or he would get himself in big trouble. Scout had cyber mailed him often with news of Karu. Karu and Scout cyber phoned each other during the summer and Reeny was always brought up in the conversation. Scout sounded exasperated at the two when she contacted Reeny on the cyber phone toward the end of the vacation. Reeny thought Scout sounded more mature and she certainly had gotten even prettier. When he turned on the computer phone and there was her face staring at him, he could not believe the change. She, of course had to joke with him about Karu. Even though she acted put out, he knew she enjoyed the intrigue. He was thinking of a good practical joke he could play on her when they got back into space.

Jon and Hannah had kept in touch all of the vacation. Reeny envied Jon his quick access to his girlfriend. Reeny knew better then to even try to contact Karu directly. He was told this would get her parents upset and may cause them to move her to the other side of the planet. He did not want that to happen. Reeny did not know what he was going to do about seeing Karu when he got back. He hated having to sneak over the canal all the time. He was going to have to find a better way to deal with this.

Chapter 10

The Space Station was abuzz in activity. Ameriland students were everywhere and greeting each other. Parents were catching up with other parents. Reeny and Max were truly blessed to have the circle of family about them. Both sets of grandparents had come to see them off. Kay always thought how nice it was of the brothers to indulge the grandparents as they fussed over them with hugs and kisses. Grandparents could get away with that with teenagers, but parents were off limits with the kisses at that age. Kay had prepared herself for this for a long time and she thought herself doing well with the situation. There were lots of tears in the station, some parents seeing children off for the first time. Kay knew it got a little easier, but not much.

"We are so proud of the boys, Kay," Kay's sister Lynn was saying. Lynn had two married children, and one son who was very close to Reeny's age. They had grown up together. They were at each other's house when they were small. Where Reeny had a scientific mind, Cal had a musical one. Cal was in a Christian band and flew from state to state, and enjoyed a degree of popularity. Kay was just as proud of him as Lynn was of Reeny and Max. Kay saw Cal over with the boys talking. Cal was getting ready to start his last tour this year before school started.

The good-byes were said and they boarded the ship. Kay was telling herself to hang on a little longer. She saw Jon's parents and waved them over. Joyce was fresh from crying and Ed looked a little sad. Jon was their only child and Kay wondered what it was like for them to go home to an empty house. Without Luke she and Vince would be in that position.

"Joyce and Ed, you have met my family haven't you?" Kay was asking. She waved them on over toward the family. Everyone exchanged greetings.

"Kay how was your summer?" Joyce asked.

"Oh, it was about the same, a lot of activities with the boys and their friends. We enjoy the boys at home and I wish they could be here and have the same education." Despite what the boys put her through, she meant that with all of her heart.

"I know, I feel the same way," Joyce replied, and Kay put her arm around her to comfort her. She saw Vince over talking to Ed. Ed loved to talk about rockets with Vince.

They all moved toward the window for take-off. Luke was studying the old Space Hubble photos on the wall and Vince had to pull him away to watch the take-off. It was a spectacular take-off. The view was wonderful and it never ceased to fascinate the crowd. They waved, even though no one could see them at that point. It was for their own good-byes and a way to let go.

All were making their way toward the exits. Kay and Vince said good-bye to Joyce and Ed. Kay was deep in her thoughts again.

"Mom, Mom!" Luke had gotten loud by the time Kay turned around to acknowledge him.

"What is it Luke?" Kay asked.

"I want something to drink," Luke whined.

"All right go to your dad, he has the money card." Kay was thinking of all the things she forgot to tell the boys. They would call twice while in flight. She was already looking forward to the com calls.

The kids were seated in flight chairs until take-off was over and the signal was given that they could go to the rooms. They were all headed that way laughing and talking loudly. They were told to be quieter by the hall monitors.

"Hey, Jon I got something we can do," Reeny said in a low voice.

"Yeah, like what?" Jon asked back in a skeptical tone. He hoped Reeny wasn't going to start them into trouble. He did not want to pull latrine or garbage duty this early in the trip.

"Do you want to get Scout for all her teasing?"

"Like how?"

"I got some green dye, it is pretty good stuff. After all of us get to the gathering room at 11:00, we will sneak out. We will set this up over her door and when she walks in, 'kaboom!' The dye will stay with her for a while, but it's harmless," Reeny explained.

"How do you know Hannah won't go in first?" Jon asked.

"That is where you step in. You make sure Hannah is distracted." Reeny sounded like he had it all planned out.

After settling in, they all met in the gathering room at the appointed time. They were chattering away before Mr. Halbrook got up to settle them down and give the usual flight speech. It was the usual run-down of rules and safety procedures. Reeny and Jon could have used this refresher speech more then anyone, but they were on their way to Scout's room.

"Are you sure this stuff will come off pretty good?" Jon asked.

"Yeah, she can wash it out. It might take a couple of washings, but I don't want to be mean to Scout. She will laugh at it," Reeny said as they reached the door.

"I hear footsteps. Quick, get inside!" Jon said, frantic.

Reeny rigged the container up over the door and closed it gently as he stepped into the hall. Jon was still unsure about it.

"Ok, I fixed it where it will just splash a little out. I didn't want to pour any of it down their sink, so it is still full. We can get the rest later," Reeny said.

They went back to the gathering room and stayed in the back until Mr. Halbrook finished the speech. They found the girls in the crowd and asked if they could walk with them to the room. Scout was suspicious of Reeny. He was too nice. Jon was walking farther behind with Hannah and telling her about some of the new virtual programs that had been added. Reeny stopped at the door with Scout.

"Well, I guess I'll be on my way," Reeny said as Scout opened the door. She opened it all the way, but nothing happened. Reeny stepped in a little to see what happened to the container, and at that time the wire broke sending the container full of dye on top of Reeny, splattering a good deal of it on Scout. Jon and Hannah had gotten too close and they got splattered. All of them were surprised and their mouths were open, but no sound came out. The liquid was cold and shocked them for a moment. When they got to their senses, Scout was the first to scream and laugh. They were all laughing and smearing it on each other. When they landed in the dark room, they gasped. They realized they were glowing in the dark.

"Reeny, I thought you said this stuff was harmless. We are glowing like glow worms!" Jon exclaimed.

Reeny turned on the light to read the container and his eyes got big. He realized he had gotten glow-in-the-dark super, super dye. He handed it to the group to see and they all rolled their eyes in disbelief.

The girls spent the evening washing and washing. They were sure the boys were doing the same. Scout thought it was funny at first, but she was getting frustrated. Hannah was silently scrubbing away. They managed to get a good deal out before it was time for chapel. The boys were outside the girl's room when they opened the door. Scout laughed when she saw them. They had not done a very good job of getting the dye off.

"We decided to make it a joke. We will all walk in the chapel together, as if we meant to do this," Reeny said.

This is one of the things Scout admired about Reeny. He had the ability to turn things around and make the best of it. Together they walked toward the chapel. They got a lot of attention along the way and when they arrived inside, Max did a double take when he saw Reeny. The Chaplain got up to speak and cleared his voice to get the attention away from the foursome. He would deal with them later. Right now he chose to ignore them. The kids were making an occasional funny remark to them, but the Chaplain was making sure he would be heard. When the ceremony came to an end and it was time for the candle lighting, the lights were turned out. There were ooh's and aah's throughout the chapel as they all turned their eyes on the glowing four bodies in the back.

Chaplain Wilkins caught the four as they were headed out the door. They found themselves face to face with him in his office. Reeny had been in his office for various reasons he cared not to discuss, but the others were looking around. Chaplain Wilkins

111

had a passion for old Earth relics from the old west days. He had cowboy hats lining the room, ropes hanging around, old photos, and a horse saddle on display. The kids were studying the décor when Chaplain Wilkins again cleared his voice, a habit he had when he was going to get serious.

"Well, I must say we had a 'glowing' experience in chapel today. I hope it was worth the trouble you went through to carry this off." Chaplain Wilkins looked straight at Reeny when he said the last sentence. He knew the brain behind this. Jon sunk deeper into his chair, and Hannah's face was turning redder making the combination of red and green quite a sight. Scout was still on the verge of laughing and Reeny just wanted Chaplain Wilkins to get on with the speech and punishment.

"I think probably cleaning duty for a week will cure any need to change your color again this trip. We will consult with Beta on what duties will be assigned to you. No call home will be necessary." Chaplain Wilkins continued talking, but none of them heard him. Images of "Big Bad Beta" were stuck in their heads. No one wanted to mess with Beta. She was a true Amerilander. She was tall, dark and scary. She had the extra fingers, and because she wore sandals, you could also see her extra toes. She was as big around as she was tall. Her temper matched her image and the kids steered clear of her. She was in charge of housekeeping, and when certain rules were broken the kids were given over to her to learn a lesson by working it off. It was very effective. The chaplain wrapped up his speech and sent the four on their way.

"Way to go Reeny. Look what we are doing now for a week. I should never listen to you," Jon said punching Reeny on the arm. Hannah was crying a little and Scout was laughing.

"Oh, lighten up Jon, we will give old big Beta a time." Scout finally stopped laughing and was trying to make everyone feel better about the situation. Reeny was quiet.

"You obviously have not met big Beta, Scout," Jon said.

"No, but I've heard of her and I think we could give her the runaround." Scout said.

"No, Scout, I've dealt with her before, there is no getting around this," Reeny spoke up.

"Well, we will make the most of it," Scout said.

They reported to housekeeping the next morning with old clothes, ready to work. They were ushered into the outer office by little

Miko. Miko was a kind little Amerilander who worked for Beta. He was always trying to soften the punishment when the kids got into trouble. He observed their green faces and turned away, not wanting to laugh.

"Well, I wish she would hurry. I don't like sitting here waiting. It just makes me more nervous," Hannah was saying, as Scout was busy looking through her pouch. Scout never went anywhere without her pouch of goodies she hung off her waist. She had everything in there. She was fishing out some lip moisture, because her lips were dry. She brought the stick out of the pouch, but it fell out of her hand and rolled across the room and out the door. Scout went after it on her hands and knees. She heard a flopping sound coming near her and looked over. She could only focus on the fat feet with twelve toes coming toward her. The flip flopping fat feet came to a halt right in front of her. Her eyes followed the heavy breathing upwards into the meanest face Scout had ever seen.

"Young lady, I see you are already in the position to do the work I'm going to give you. Scrubbing all the green dye off the floor will be the start of the day," Beta said with her arms folded as she was patting her big foot on the floor. She looked around at the rest of the crew. "We will get to work now!" With that the foursome jumped to their feet.

They found themselves still scrubbing into the evening with very little rest. The green dye was stubborn and they had to paint the wall around Scout's and Hannah's room. They complained a little, but joked a lot. One thing was certain. These kids would go to bed and sleep well tonight.

Max had sought out Reeny earlier that day to see what had happened to him. He found him in the break room in the housekeeping section. They had all stopped for a few minutes to eat and rest. They were joking around when Max entered the room.

"Well, big brother, your reputation precedes you," Max was saying as he entered the room.

"Oh, hello Max." Reeny did not say anything else hoping Max would leave. He did not want to deal with his pesky brother right now. Scout, however was interested in Max. She had heard about Max, and being curious in nature, wanted to know how he ticked.

"Max, I'm Scout. Your brother is being rude for some reason." Scout turned to give Reeny a hard look. "This is Hannah, and you know Jon."

"Hey Jon, I see you were roped into another of my brother's wild ideas," Max said.

He looked over at Hannah and nodded. Hannah again blushed.

"Without your brother my life would be normal, maybe even dull," Jon said.

"See, I'm good for something," Reeny said. At that time a noise could be heard and the group knew what it was. Heavy breathing and footsteps were lumbering down the hall toward the room. Everyone jumped up to leave, but the shadow across the threshold told them it was too late. The shadow was followed by big Beta. With one last big labored breath she bellowed, "Get to work, or you will have another day added on to your week!" All five kids went flying out the door.

"Max, why are you running? You're not in trouble." Scout was laughing as she was asking Max.

"I know, but that is one scary lady. I hope I don't get to meet her again." Max continued to follow the others until he knew there was a distance between him and that big Beta. He said his good-byes happily and went to meet his new friends. They were going to the virtual circus.

The virtual circus was a novel idea, because nearly a thousand years ago, the real circus idea began to collapse. The animal rights groups had shut down every circus that existed by lawsuits and other means. Right or wrong, they ceased to exist. With the virtual reality circus, everything could be programmed in the computer system. The images appeared real and the performances of the animals were as good as at the old circus. Since no live animals were ever used, this made everyone happy. The virtual circus now was as popular as the circus of old.

Max enjoyed eating cotton candy and seeing the elephants. He had also met a girl, and he thought she was the most wonderful thing that existed. He was watching her across the aisle while at the circus. She had a cute laugh. He hoped he could make her laugh like that when and if they were ever together. He was unsure of himself right now. When she did look over at him, he dropped his popcorn. He had met her earlier, so he felt free to go over and greet her. She asked him if he would be able to sit next to her since there was an empty seat. He was feeling pretty good about himself when he went back to his room that evening. Any apprehension he had had earlier about this trip had just been dissolved by someone called Summer Faye Williams.

Reeny decided to make his call home the second night into his work detail. He knew his mother was waiting to hear from them. When he got to the computer phone,

Max was waiting for him. They had decided on this time to be here so they could both speak to their parents. The phone made the connection and on the screen was their mom and dad with smiling faces.

"Hey Mom and Dad, What's up?" Reeny spoke first. Max had a hard time for a moment. He did not realize how hard it was going to be to see his parents. It had suddenly come to him how far away he was from home. He choked up. Reeny looked over and knew exactly how Max was feeling. He had had this feeling many times when he looked into his parents' faces.

"It gets easier Max," Reeny whispered.

"What did you say Reeny?" Kay asked.

"Oh nothing Mom, I was just saying something to Max," Reeny replied.

"Well how is the flight going so far? Are you having fun?" Vincent asked.

"Yes Dad, we are checking out some new stuff," Reeny said. Max still was not talking. Kay thought she knew why.

"Max, are you meeting new friends?" Kay asked.

"Yes Mom, there are a lot of neat people. Reeny has taken up a new hobby, he is painting." Max looked over at Reeny who was giving him a hard look.

"I did not know you were interested in painting Reeny," Kay said.

"Oh I sort of fell into it, you might say," Reeny said and kicked his brother under the desk. Max was about to laugh. Kay knew something was up, but decided not to go any further with that conversation. They talked on for several minutes until the time was up and they had to say good-bye. It was hard, the first phone call back home after summer break always was. Max had to leave quickly because he felt tears coming and he did not want Reeny to see him.

When they hung up Kay and Vince had a moment to reflect on what was said.

"Do you think Reeny felt good? Did he seem all right to you?" Kay asked Vince.

"Yes, he looked fine. Why?"

"I don't know, but his face looked a little green. I hope he is not coming down with some stomach virus," Kay said.

"Maybe it was the picture we were getting," Vince said.

"Max's face did not look green," Kay replied back.

"I don't know, but I'm more worried about Max. He looked a little lost," Vince said.

"Yes I know, but Reeny is there and he will take care of him. Maybe Reeny will start setting a good example and stay out of trouble," Kay said.

"Speaking of trouble, what happen today at school with Luke?" Vince asked.

"I got a call from the teacher. I wish they would call you for a change. Luke was in the middle of a food fight. When a stray tomato hit him, he seemed to think it was time to get into the fight. He has silent lunch for a week and lunchroom duties after his lunch every day for three days." Kay rolled her eyes over at Vince.

"Don't give me that look," Vince said.

"What look?" Kay asked with an innocent voice.

"The 'I don't want to deal with this, you deal with this' look," Vince said. Kay just looked at him and finally he got up to go talk to Luke.

"Luke, you missed your brothers' com call. We tried to find you. Where were you?" Vince was asking Luke as he entered his room. Luke was busy playing a virtual hand-held game. He took the gear off his head to talk to his Dad.

"Whatever they said, it is not true," Luke said immediately.

"Whatever who said?" Vince asked.

"You know, the teachers."

"I don't know. I wasn't the one who talked to the teachers." Vince wondered where this conversation was going.

"Oh, they called Mom again. She is probably mad, but it wasn't my fault. I was just sitting there minding my own business and out of nowhere a tomato smacked me."

"Let me get this straight. Out of nowhere a tomato hit you." Vince was trying to get to the bottom of this situation. Luke had poked out his lip and was nodding.

"All right, what did you do?" Vince asked.

"Well I did what anyone would do, I wiped it off and it stuck on my hand. When I tried to shake the tomato off my hand, it just flew across the room and into Julie's hair. She had to go and scream. Next thing I knew, ole Mr. Rogers was telling me I was in trouble. Now I have silent lunch and lunch duties." Luke sounded pretty convincing, but years of experience told Vince this wasn't the whole story.

"Oh my, they gave you silent lunch for wiping off a tomato," Vince said, with a lot of doubt in his voice. Luke caught on and decided to look pitiful. He knew he could look pretty good, because he practiced these looks in the mirror. He had all the looks down pat, now was time to bring out the, "I didn't mean to," look. He didn't think it was working, so he tried to add tears. Dad was standing with his hands on his hips. This meant nothing was going to work and he was in for it.

"I think this weekend we will not have friends over. This is the second phone call this week from the school."

"Dad, you're not going to have friends over either, what did you do?"

"Luke, don't get cute with me. You know what I mean."

"Oh all right, I'll just sit around and look out at the trees and think about my friends and what I could be doing. They get into trouble, but they don't get punished like I do. Their parents have mercy on them. They believe them." Luke was playing it for what it was worth.

"Sorry Luke, this isn't working. I'm going to talk to Mom. I hope all your homework is finished. I don't want any more calls from the teacher," Vince said and shook his head as he headed back to the den.

When Vince caught up with Kay in the kitchen, he was laughing.

"I think you should sign Luke up for acting classes," Vince said.

"Did he try every trick in the book to get out of trouble?" Kay asked.

"He always does, and you know nothing is ever his fault."

"No of course not, he is the innocent victim," Kay laughed.

After hearing from the brothers, both Kay and Vince were in a lighter mood. They always felt better when they were in contact with their kids. They needed to feel like all was well with their world and that everything was going along at a good pace. Kay was a little worried about Max, but in her heart she was at peace about things.

"You know that wormhole in space they discovered a couple of years ago?" Vince asked.

"Yes, the one they were going to research to check out the stability of it. Do they have more news on it?"

"Yeah, they are pretty sure it is stable and will stay the same size. They might start using it soon. It will knock off a week of travel to Ameriland if it is permanent," Vince said.

"Honey, that is great news. Wormholes are so unpredictable. I did not get my hopes up. Maybe they can use this and it will put us one week closer to our sons." Kay was happier that evening than she had been in a while. All new discoveries that could lessen the miles between her and her boys were good news.

Chapter 11

Reeny and the others finished their duties for big Beta and were celebrating by going to the virtual theater. They saw a good show and went to get something to eat. They caught up with some gossip from the others, since they had practically been isolated for two weeks.

"Hey Reeny, heard you have been big Beta's slave for a while. Been seeing green lately?" Some of the boys were taunting the four at the table and laughing. Reeny and Scout laughed with everyone, but Jon and Hannah were embarrassed. Max came walking in when all this was going on and found it funny. He also observed his big brother and learned how Reeny handled things. He admired Reeny because he seemed not to lose his cool. He was proud to be his brother, but he would never say that to Reeny, at least not until they were grown.

"Jon, lets go to the interactive virtual theater tomorrow night. We will program a movie to act in ourselves," Reeny said.

"I don't know. I only do virtual theater at home. I don't like an audience," Jon said.

"Yeah, but this is more fun. It makes it more real because the space is bigger. Why don't you try it just once? I'm sure you will like it." Reeny was sure Jon would like it. Scout was listening closely to the conversation.

"Can we come along?" Scout asked.

"Sure, do you want to be part of the program?" Reeny asked.

"No, I think we will just watch," Scout said, but Hannah detected something was going on in Scout's head by the tone of her voice. The boys continued to make plans and did not notice.

The next evening Jon and Reeny had programmed their movie. It was going to be about the old west in America. Reeny had always been interested in that time. They had found a movie they could interact with as cowboys. The program works by placing themselves in the hologram movie. They choose the character they want to be and the program eliminates the hologram version of that character to make room for the real person. One has to learn the part of the character in order to interact with the other hologram figures. Things can be written and added into some of the programs. Reeny chose a program he could add his own story in. Scout, Hannah and some of the other kids settled in to watch what Reeny and Jon had been working on for hours.

Reeny was in the middle of a gunfight, when things started to look different from what he had programmed in. At first it was little things, like a dog running across the set. Then it was birds flying all over the place, but the thing that got him was the elephant that lumbered in, raised his truck and bellowed. He suspected who was behind this before he looked out into the audience. Scout was rolling. She had successfully reprogrammed the movie and she was proud of herself. Everyone was laughing at Reeny and Jon, who were trying to deal with this elephant and the birds flying around. Reeny had to hand it to Scout, she said she would get him back and she did. They all had a good laugh going back to the rooms that night. Jon was thinking he would never try that again.

Chapter 12

Before long the flight was over and the students were back in their rooms, catching up on news from the Amerilanders. There was talk of political unrest on Russo, but the students did not give it much thought. The Russo students seemed a little unsettled at first, but continued their routine at the school. For the most part, peace had reigned in the worlds for many years. There had only been a few small skirmishes, but no war for years. When one had not seen war on a large scale, it was hard to comprehend and it was hard to see that it might come. Ameriland had added some new space ships to the flight school. They were made for wartime with firepower and quick maneuverability. Eyebrows were raised when they were added to the flight school, because the school dealt mostly with exploration. The American government felt this was a good idea, citing there were rumblings of discontent among certain factions on Russo. They had their spies and they had been watching the situation for years. Ameriland could be vulnerable if any war on Russo broke out. They wanted the

Ameriland students headed to flight school to learn how to operate these new ships.

Most students were eighteen when they could enter flight school. When Reeny heard about the new ships, he wanted more then ever to go to flight school. He was sixteen and would have to wait two years unless he could figure out another way. He was discussing it with Jon, who also was interested.

"Look, we might as well face it. They won't consider us until we are at least seventeen, and then we would have to pass some pretty hard tests. Only a few seventeen-year-olds are admitted," Jon said.

"Then we had better start figuring out those tests and what we need to pass. I want to be there by next year," Reeny replied.

"I see you have your mind made up." Jon knew what he would be in for the next year until Reeny got what he was after. Jon also knew Reeny would drag him along. Max had heard about the new space ships and asked Reeny what he thought was going on. Reeny did not know any more than anyone else, but Reeny had a way of sensing things to come. Reeny, now more then ever, wanted to be in flight school.

Reeny had managed once to see Karu since he had returned to school. He was going to try to go see her again. This time he decided to take the direct approach, and see her at her parent's house the next weekend she was home. He wanted to talk to her about flight school and the uneasy feeling he had lately. He hoped that if he could just meet her parents, they might not be so opposed to him. He discussed his plan with Scout over the computer phone. She thought the plan might just work, but she had a better one.

"Why don't you come with me to visit Karu next weekend? I often go to her house when she goes home. They won't think anything of your coming with me. They might even, you know, like you." And she made a gagging sound and laughed.

"That would be a good idea. I'm surprised you thought of it," Reeny said.

"Oh you're so smart," Scout teased back.

"Well, give me the details. How do I meet up with you?" Reeny asked.

"We will meet at the canal pier Saturday morning around 10:00. We will then ride Pubcan Rt. 10. There is a stop within walking distance of her house," Scout finished.

"All right, I'll be there," Reeny said, thinking Scout must have been figuring this out for a while.

"Hey, I hear you want to join flight school by next year. Are you itching to get into those new ships?" Scout asked.

"Yeah, as a matter of fact I am," Reeny said.

"I'm interested too. I might just try for next year myself," Scout said.

"You? Scout, these are war machines. I thought you were going for space exploration." Reeny was surprised at what he was hearing.

"I was until I read about these space ships. I'm as excited as you are. My parents don't like the idea."

"You have already discussed this with your parents?"

"Yes, last night. They have heard some things about Russo. They don't want their little girl involved with war."

"I don't blame them, but it probably won't come to war. Well I've got to go. I have a meeting in a few. See ya," Reeny said.

"Yeah, Saturday," Scout said

Hannah had been in the room the last few minutes. She did not mean to pry, but had heard some of the conversation.

"Hey Scout, are you ready to go eat?" Hannah asked.

"Oh, hey Hannah. I did not hear you come in."

"Where is Karu?" Hannah asked.

"She ate earlier. She had some studying to do. She left for the library a while ago," Scout replied.

"Do you really plan on entering the flight school just so you can get in one of those new ships?" Hannah asked.

"Oh, so you heard. Well I'm keeping it no secret. The fact is, this is what I've been waiting for. This could be exciting."

"Scout, this could mean being in a war."

"Yes, I know."

"Doesn't that worry you?"

"No, for some reason I am not worried. I just know this is right for me," Scout was saying as she finished getting ready to go.

"I would think about it more if I were you," Hannah said as she followed her out the door.

"Well, I have a year at least. They won't let any of us in flight school until we are seventeen. You know how hard it is to get in at seventeen. It is worth a try," Scout said with conviction in her voice.

"By the way, I'm going to take Reeny to Karu's house this weekend," Scout said daringly.

131

"Scout you are full of surprises and you are awfully brave. I could not be half as brave as you are," Hannah said.

"Hannah, you just need to be yourself. You will be surprised how brave you can be when you have to be." Scout always seemed to say the right thing, and that was another thing to be admired in her.

Chapter 13

Max was studying the candy machine in the study-hall building. He had forgotten his code for the machine and was thinking hard. He really wanted some candy and he started fooling with the buttons. Before he knew it candy was spewing out everywhere. Everyone was laughing and grabbing the candy. Max was trying to pick up the candy as fast as he could. He did not know what he was going to do. While he was picking up the candy, he heard everyone leaving the room in a hurry. As a shadow fell over him, he slowly looked around and his eyes went upward. There standing over him was the biggest, meanest-looking Russo he had ever seen. The third eye was particularly piercing.

"Uh, who are you?" Max asked, knowing he was not a teacher or an administrator. He wore some sort of work uniform, but Max thought this man must have some authority.

"I'm Uno, and who are you, and why did you break the candy machine?" Uno asked in his booming voice.

"I'm Max Gallager, uh I'm new here. I forgot my code, but I did not mean to break the machine." Max was looking sheepish.

Uno rolled his third eye and said, "So another Gallager. Well, I might have known. You are Reeny's younger brother. You will probably get to know me pretty well. First you're going to pick this candy up, and then we will talk about how you will work this off. Come see me in my office. I'm in building C, room 210. I will meet you there in an hour," Uno said as he walked out the door.

Max slapped his hand to his forehead and mumbled to himself. How could he be so stupid? Reeny had talked of Uno many times. He knew he could be rough, but Reeny had always said he was fair. Reeny admired Uno and had said so. He would have to hurry to get all this candy up and eat something before he met with Uno. He did not know what was in store for him, so he wanted to talk to Reeny.

Reeny laughed when he heard Max's story. He told Max not to worry about Uno.

"Uno's bark is bigger then his bite, Max," Reeny said.

"What do you think I'll have to do, and will they call Mom and Dad?" Max asked concerned. It was too early to bother the parents.

"Uno doesn't tell on anyone unless it is really serious. He has the authority to punish for things that pertain to property damage and will give a lecture if he sees you doing something lame. Uno can be your friend if you give him respect. It is best to get on the good side of him," Reeny said.

Max went on his way to Uno's office feeling a little better about things. Max was still unsure of his surroundings and was treading lightly. Max was that way until he got to know his way around. He would probably find many things to get into before he graduated, and some of them would not be so good.

The next day Max was cleaning out the storage room, one of his many jobs for the week, when he heard voices behind him.

"Hi, Max." Max turned around and there was Summer Faye. He could not believe his bad luck. What would she think?

"Hi, Summer Faye." He did not know what else to say.

"I heard what happened, that is too bad. Will you be free Saturday?"

"Yes, I'm just doing this until Friday," Max replied.

"Can you come to the park with a bunch of us? We heard about the Kaltos and wanted to see them. Have you seen them yet?"

"No, Reeny talked about them some. I did want to see them. What are the plans?"

"We are going to meet at the park at 11:00 in the morning. We ought to be able to see some of them. We are not allowed to get close, it is the school rules." Summer Faye was talking and Max started laughing.

"What are you laughing at?" Summer Faye asked.

"School rules hah, I plan to ride those monsters."

"You can't be serious, the females are supposed to be aggressive. You could get hurt."

"Only if you mess with the females that just had babies. Reeny told me all about it. It will be fun. They have races," Max said.

"I don't think I will go anywhere near them, I'm just curious about them. This being my first year here, I guess I have a lot to see," Summer Faye was saying as Max began to work again. She saw Uno coming and she could not take her eyes off of him.
He stopped in front of her and she gulped.

"Oh, Summer Faye this is Uno," Max said busying himself some more. He did not want Uno to think he had not been working.

"Hi, uh how are you?" She reached out to shake hands. Uno grabbed her hand and shook it hard and gave her a grin, and the third eye gave a wink. Summer Faye was at a loss for more words. This was the first time she had seen a Russo with the third eye up close. She certainly knew they existed, but it was still a shock. Before she knew it, Uno walked on past and down the hall.

"He is scary," Summer Faye said.

"Yes, he scared me at first too, but he's all right," Max said.

"I guess I had better go, see ya Saturday."

"Yeah, I'll come," Max said as he watched Summer Faye go down the hall. He felt weak at the knees. He could not believe the prettiest girl in the place had actually asked him out. That is what he thought she did anyway. Maybe she was just being nice. He hoped she actually liked him.

He went to his room that night full of dreams about Saturday. He pictured himself the hero of the day. He would ride the big, forbidden Kaltos and win the race. He could picture Summer Faye's face all alight with awe.

"What is that silly grin you have on your face Max?" It was Larry speaking. Larry had become a friend to Max. He was one the few African Americans on Ameriland. Larry liked Max's spirit right off the bat. Max knew Larry had some adventure in him and quickly took to him.

"Oh, I don't know, maybe I'm just happy," Max said.

"OK, I just came to see if you wanted to go do something." Larry wasn't going to tease Max anymore, but he knew something was up.

"No, actually I'm pretty tired. I'm just going to stay in."

"Uno works you hard uh?"

"No, he is not too bad. He got me this great sandwich for lunch and gave me breaks. He can be nice."

"That's good to know. He sure looks mean. Well I'm going to catch up with the others, see you later." Larry walked out of the room and waved.

"Yeah, I'll see you." Max waved back. He then got back to his daydreams.

Saturday came around quickly for Max. He had not had a chance to talk to Reeny about the Kaltos. He knew Reeny had won a few races and wanted some pointers. He was in a hurry as he passed Larry in the hallway.

"Hey, where you going so fast Max? I thought you would be sleeping in this morning, seeing as you had such a hard week," Larry commented.

"Hi Larry, I'm just going down to the field. Some people are having a picnic there in a few minutes. I sort of promised to be there, like right now," Max said as he pushed the button on his hologram watch. He had a whimsical watch that was so popular. When the button is pushed a hologram cartoon comes up out of the watch and tells the time and makes a joke. Max's watch had hundreds of jokes programmed in. He laughed at every one. Larry laughed at the joke too.

"Maybe I'll come later. I have to do some stuff right now. It would be all right wouldn't it?" Larry asked.

"Oh sure, you don't have to have an engraved invitation. The field is for everyone," Max said as he took off down the hall.

Max arrived a little late and everyone was eating. Summer Faye saw him coming and went out to greet him. He saw her coming and his heart beat faster. She took his breath away. Summer Faye's Hispanic heritage was prominent. Her flawless skin, dark hair and the deepest brown eyes he had ever seen seemed to be altogether too much for a young lad to take in. He just stood there with his mouth open as she handed him some food and gave him a great big smile.

"Come on over, we saw some Kaltos down by the trees a few minutes ago," Summer Faye said.

"Really, I'll have to check them out as soon as I eat. Do you want to get closer to them?" Max asked.

"No, I'm staying up here on the hill. They don't come up this far often, so I'm told," Summer Faye said with a little nervous voice.

"They don't come after people usually," said Max.

"Yes I know, but they are big and fierce looking," Summer Faye said.

Max looked up to see Reeny and Jon coming across the field heading toward where the Kaltos were seen. He put down his sandwich and started toward them, leaving Summer Faye puzzled at his sudden departure.

"Reeny!" Max yelled as he was catching up with Reeny. "Where you going? He really knew the answer, but asked anyway.

"We're going to catch some young Kaltos and race," Reeny said.

"Is it safe?" Max asked apprehensively.

"Sure, if you race the young ones. You have to keep away from the nest, but that is easy to do. They are deep in the wood usually," Reeny replied.

"I want to try," Max said.

"Max, you had better start with a real little one. You can get thrown and trampled if you don't get the hang of it," Reeny said with some authority.

"Oh give me a break. I can do this if you can, big shot!" Max shot back.

"Well Reeny, I think we had better step aside. We have new competition," Jon said.

"Look Max, I can't let you get hurt. Mom and Dad would get me good. You need to listen to me," Reeny said.

"You're kidding, right? You think you're in charge of me? Forget it! I'm old enough to take care of myself. So just show me the Kaltos, I'm ready to ride," Max replied.

"All right, but if you get hurt, I'm not taking the blame." Reeny wasn't going to argue. Max was too much like him in that respect. Reeny knew he would do what he wanted to do.

"Look, there are some nice-looking Kaltos over there. Let's round them up," Jon said as he clapped his hands toward the Kaltos so he could get them where he wanted them. Some of the kids were watching from the hill, among them was Summer Faye. This was not lost on Max as he gazed in her direction. He was determined to make an impression. He followed Reeny and Jon's lead and began to round up the Kaltos. They were

able to get three fair-sized males, and they led
them to an outlined area on the field. The
kids had outlined the race boundaries years
ago when the first group of students started
racing Kaltos. It had been a tradition since
the school opened. There had been a few
serious accidents and racing was banned by
the school, but the students did it anyway.
True to the nature of teenagers, they think
nothing will happen to them. Sometimes they
were caught and punished, but most of the
time they got away with it. Max had been
given all the rules for Ameriland Students and
he was aware that he was breaking a rule.
Reeny had always raced, so he was going for
it. They got the Kaltos on the line and Reeny
and Jon hoped up on theirs. Max did the
same, but slid off the side. He had not
jumped high enough, so he tried it again. He
jumped higher and grabbed the hard mane-
like structure lining the monster's neck. He
held on tight. Reeny looked over worried, but
decided not to say anything. Jon rolled his
eyes and shook his head. Some of the
students on the hill had laughed, but most of
the others admired the boys for their bravery.
Summer Faye however was biting her lip. She
wanted to look away and dared not. She felt
that if she could keep her eyes on Max, he
would be fine.

"OK, Let's see what these monsters can do! Go!" Jon yelled, and with that the Kaltos took off. Reeny's was ahead when Max looked over. He was determined to win at all costs, so he gave a jab to the side of his Kalto. The Kalto reared up and took off past Jon and Reeny and across the finish line. Max looked back at the others who were dumbfounded at the outcome. Reeny was used to winning, and he did not take losing very well.

"You should watch out with these Kaltos, you don't want to make them mad. You are lucky to still be on top of that monster!" Reeny yelled at his brother.

"Oh be quiet. I won and you are just sore. Get over it!" Max yelled back as he dismounted the beast. The boys let the Kaltos go and started walking up the hill.

"Let's see you do that tonight," Jon said.

"Jon, nothing's going on tonight," Reeny said as he poked him with his elbow and gave him a look to hush him.

"What's happening tonight? I can see something is up, what is it?" Max asked.

"Do you think today was the real race? We were just practicing, and, you know, picking out some nice Kaltos," Jon said and shrugged his shoulders toward Reeny who was staring at him in exasperation.

143

"Don't encourage him Jon.   He is not ready to race tonight," Reeny said.

"Oh, I just won the race and I'm not ready. Who's not ready?" Max asked.

"I believe it is called beginners luck," Reeny argued back.

"Well maybe and maybe not. What time tonight Jon?" Max turned to Jon knowing he would give him the information he needed.

"We meet at 7:00 and round up our Kaltos. We pick which ones we want and start the race at 7:30."   Jon spilled out the information readily enough, with Reeny giving him a hard look. They parted their ways when Max spotted Summer Faye coming toward him.

"See ya tonight." Jon gave a wave and loped off.

"Way to go Jon," Reeny said when they were out of earshot of the others.

"He'll learn his lesson," Jon said.

"Yes and his ego will probably be hurt the most," Reeny said as he glanced back and saw the object of his brother's affections and the force behind the need to race Kaltos. He understood this and wanted to be able to warn his little brother.   He knew he would not listen, so he shook his head and continued on.

Summer Faye was gushing over Max. Max was smiling and proud that he got the result he wanted. He was thinking he did not really want to race tonight, but his big mouth got him into it. He had not realized how scary being on top of one of those beasts could be. He had almost fallen off a couple of times, and did not know if his luck or his guardian angel would come through for him again. Maybe if Reeny made a bigger deal of it, he would give in and not race. He could blame it on Reeny and save face.

"Wow, you looked like you've raced Kaltos before. You won! It was pretty scary. How did it feel up that high on something like that?" Summer Faye was excited and talking 90 miles a minute. This was one of the most exciting days she had had since she arrived at the school, and she wasn't letting the moment pass. Everyone crowded around Max and asked about the ride. Some of them wanted to try it. They were all first year students and did not know too much about Kaltos. Max passed through the crowd in a daze, wondering what to do about the mess he had gotten into trying to impress a girl. Why did he do this to himself? After he stayed and talked with the others, he finished eating, said good-bye to Summer Faye, and went looking for Reeny.

Some of the other boys were standing around the hall when he arrived at Reeny's room. He looked in the room and Jon was working on something with his virtual computer. "Where is Reeny?" Max said looking around.

"Shut the door and I will tell you," Jon said looking toward the group outside his door. Max, wondering what was going on, obeyed and shut the door.

"What's up?" Max asked.

"Reeny went with Scout to see Karu at her parent's house across the channel," Jon said with a low voice.

"Who's Karu, and what is all the secrecy?" Max said as Jon put his hand up to make him lower his voice.

"You don't know about Karu? Boy, Reeny does keep things to himself. She is his girlfriend and an Amerilander," Jon said, wondering if he would be in trouble with Reeny over this.

"Wow, Reeny has a girlfriend and she is an Amerilander? Does she have six fingers and six toes?" Max was excited to hear this kind of news about his brother.

"No, she has mostly Earth features. She is good looking," Jon replied.

"Why do we have to keep quiet about it? Why is Reeny tight lipped about a pretty girlfriend? He would normally be bragging. What's the deal?" Max asked.

"The parents don't approve of an Earthling dating their daughter. Their ways are different," Jon said.

"How different can they be? I mean, I know they have a history of not mixing with Earthlings, but I thought things had changed." Max had studied the history of Ameriland and remembered quite a bit.

"In the last few years the boundaries have come down, but I'm afraid for some of the more devout families, it is still the same."

"And Karu's family is one of these families?" Max asked.

"Yes, they are politically strong and wealthy."

"Reeny knows how to pick 'um." Max had picked up a ball and was tossing it up and down. "So, what is going to happen today?" Max turned toward Jon and asked.

"Reeny thinks if he uses his charm, he will win over the parents," Jon said grabbing the ball from Max's hand.

"It's not like he will marry her or anything. I don't see the big deal," Max said.

"I know, but it is a concern to some people."

"Could he get into trouble, you know, seeing her and all?

"Could, if the parents disapprove and contact the school. He has been sneaking

147

over the canal to the girls' school where she goes, and it was becoming more difficult. Today could end that if the parents decide to pull her out of the school because of Reeny. They could send her to the other side of the planet," Jon said.

"They would do that?"

"Yes, Karu seems to think they are capable of just that. She is very afraid to go against her parents, but she really likes Reeny."

"Sounds like too much trouble for a girl to me," Max said and his mind wondered to Summer Faye. Would he go through so much for her? Maybe. He went back to his place with a new understanding of his older brother, and a new respect. Suddenly he stopped and remembered what he had gone to see his brother about, and all the worries flooded back. The question was what to do about tonight. Maybe Reeny would not get back in time, and he could say he went searching for him. He hoped something would happen before he had to face one of those hideous creatures again. He would have to think of a way out, but if it came to racing then he would take it slower tonight. Maybe he could find a half dead Kalto or a real small one. He might still count on Reeny's persistence to get him out. He looked up at the reddish sky and over at the beautiful canal; he looked back up to see a flock of green Krito birds passing. While he gazed around, he seemed to be seeing Ameriland for the first time. As a new student, it had been hectic and frightening at times. He hardly had time to turn around, but now standing here, reality set in as he watched a big fluffy green Krito feather slowly float down in front of him. He picked it up, much in thought, as he walked on.

Reeny was nervous standing at the door of Karu's house with Scout. Scout was humming some stupid tune and he wished she would clam up. Scout looked over at him and it annoyed him.

"What?" Reeny rolled his eyes and asked Scout.

"Nothing, it's just that you have a dumb look on your face," Scout said and continued to hum. She put her hand on the I.D. computer again. The door opened and a servant answered the door. He was a tall Russonian, but not a Talcot. He bowed and said, "Hello, Ms. Scout, who is your friend?"

"Oh this is Reeny, uh we came to see Karu. Is she home?" Scout knew she was home, because she had contacted her. She gave one of her sweet winning smiles to Lul and he smiled back. He was on to her. He sensed something was up.

"Yes, come on in, I'll call her. She'll be down directly."

"Thanks Lul," Scout said, and raised her eyebrows and shrugged her shoulders at Reeny.

"I don't know if this was such a good idea now," Reeny said as his confidence was slowly leaving him.

"It will be fine," Scout said and put her hand on his back and gently shoved him forward into the room.

"Hey guys!" Karu was bouncing down the stairs. Reeny and Karu locked eyes; they were both thinking how much the other had changed. Karu saw a taller filled-out Reeny. Reeny was thinking about how much more beautiful Karu had gotten. Ameriland's climate stayed about the same all the time, it was a tropical setting and he could tell Karu had been outdoors a lot in the paradise in which she lived. Her red hair had taken on a golden tint and the green eyes shone like a cat's from beyond the tan face. When she gave him a smile, the teeth were as white as the clouds in the sky. She was in front of him before he could speak.

"Reeny, hello." It was Scout waving her hand in front of his face, bringing him out of the trance he was in. "Say something! I did not go through so much for you to just stand there." Scout was one to get to the point.

"Hi Karu." Reeny leaned forward and gave Karu a small wispy kiss on her cheek. Scout was tapping her foot and rolling her eyes.

"Let's go out into the garden, lunch will be ready soon," Karu said as they followed her out back.

"Do your parents know Reeny is with me?" Scout asked.

"Yes, they think he is just a friend," Karu said.

"Good, just play it cool," Scout said and looked over at Reeny.

"Maybe if they get to know you, they will like you," Karu said.

"Yes, he can just visit with me and come here with me until he gets to be a part of the scene. They'll get used to him and it will be great," Scout said gesturing with her arms and hands. Karu knew she did this when she was nervous. They sat down on the bench in the garden. There were beautiful plants everywhere. The smell was incredible. Reeny thought there was probably no place in the universe that held so much beauty as Ameriland. He somehow felt at home here more then on Earth. It was inexplainable.

They talked about the school and plans for activities coming up. They were laughing at the antics they played on each other during the trip back to Ameriland.

"It's amazing your faces aren't still green," Karu said, hardly getting it out, she was laughing so hard.

That evening Reeny and Jon were headed toward the field for the race.

"How was the visit at Karu's house?" Jon asked. So far he had kept still about mentioning the morning to Reeny.

"It was all right, the parents were nice and all, but I wasn't able to talk to Karu alone," Reeny said downheartedly.

"Well at least you got to see her."

"Yeah, I guess. Look, here comes Max, we have got to keep him out of this race tonight," Reeny said looking at Max waving and coming their way.

"Hey man, I thought you weren't gonna show. How was Karu? That is her name isn't it? Max asked.

"How did you know about Karu?" Reeny asked as he gave Jon a hard look. Jon shrugged.

"Oh, I have my ways," Jon was looking over Reeny's shoulder with a "don't tell look" and Max quickly changed the subject. "Well are we racing or not?" Max was hoping for a negative response.

"We are racing, not you," Reeny said firmly.

"Oh so trying to get rid of the competition uh?" Max had to make it look good. He was secretly happy with the way the conversation was going.

"Max, do whatever you want. Just don't complain to me," Reeny said.

"Well uh, I don't have to race if this will cause you to be so sore at me. Can I at least help with the round up?" Max had to save face.

"I don't see the harm in that," Jon said, and Reeny headed out in front of them shaking his head.

Some of the senior boys were already there, and Max saw them.

"I didn't know this was such a big deal," Max said to Jon.

"Yeah the older boys usually dominate the races. This is their last year and they like to go out with a bang," Jon replied.

Someone whistled and they all started to round up Kaltos. They picked the ones they wanted and lined up. No one saw the two boys, Adu and Kel, slip into the forest. They were whispering to themselves. They were Russonians with the third eyes. They were not Ameriland students, but often hung out at the field. Their parents had temporary visas and worked on the planet.

"We'll fix these Ameriland snobs good," Adu said with a sneer. "Have you got the rope?"

"Sure do," Kel answered as he pulled out the rope from under his shirt.

"Good, let's find us a big female Kalto," Adu was saying as he was looking around. Just then a bellow was heard through the trees. Both boys crouched and slowly went toward the bellow. As they moved aside the brush, the forest revealed a monster, just what the boys ordered. They shoved each other happily and got to work. They knew to tie the month together and control the tail. This done they shoved the unwilling beast toward the field. The race was under way as they got to the clearing. No one's attention was on the two scoundrels about to wreak havoc. They let the Kalto go at the edge of the field in front of those racers coming their way. It gave a frightened bellow as it flipped around and around. Reeny, who was ahead in the race, found himself right in front of the massive body. His Kalto was spooked and begin to jump out of control. Reeny held on tight but found himself thrown into the air. The other boys were being thrown all over and underneath the Kaltos. Reeny got up in time to see the thorny tail swaying toward his face. He did not remember anything else. Max dragged his limp, bleeding body to the canal. When he thought they were safe from the destruction behind him, he splashed some of the canal water on Reeny's face. Reeny came around.

"What happened?" Reeny asked, but could not figure why his month wasn't working right. Max was giving him a horrified look and his face was pale as a ghost. Reeny spit into his hand and to his disbelief he was holding some of his teeth in his hand. The scene played itself over again in his head; he felt dazed and confused. The face of Max became fuzzy as he slid into the unconscious realm. Sirens were heard in the distance and Max knew the canal patrol would be there soon. He was worried about Reeny and wondered where Jon was. The patrol pulled up to the canal deck at the edge of the field. They at first witnessed the two boys on the canal wall. One seemed to be badly hurt. They heard screaming and Kaltos bellowing from the field. The patrol quickly accessed the situation and called for more help. Two went over to Max and Reeny.

"What happened?" one patrolman asked as the other called for medical help.

"I don't know. The Kaltos went crazy," Max said.

"Kids racing Kaltos again, when will they learn?"

A patrolman was practically rolling down the hill toward the boat. "We have to get these kids help quickly. Some have been trampled. It's a mess up there." He was wiping sweat from his brow as if to wipe the horrible scene out of his mind.

The medical patrol was there in no time, picking up kids on stretchers. The scene appeared to be much worse then it was. Reeny seemed to be the one that had taken the brunt of the catastrophe. As his limp bleeding body was put on a stretcher, Max felt the biggest lump in his throat. For the very first time in his life, he thought about death seriously. Summer Faye came up behind him, but she said nothing. The kids on the hill had witnessed a nightmare and were in shock. Crying echoed in Max's ear from the field. Max grew up a bit that evening, and as he witnessed the sun setting over the canal, he knew somehow that something had changed forever. Suddenly he took off running toward the hospital. He followed the blinking lights on the canal medical boats until he lost sight of them. He continued running beside the canal, sometimes bumping into people taking strolls along the lighted canal. He stepped on the tail of an unrecognizable little beast and it squealed, but he kept going with tears streaming down, streaking his dirty face. The hospital lights could be seen in a distance, and his body was weary as his feet stumbled to the doors. There was a flurry of activity about him and his head whirled. People raced everywhere and he reached out to a motherly looking nurse, but words would not come out. "Do you have someone who was brought in tonight?" The nurse asked as she observed the frightened ghostlike appearance of the boy. He reminded her of her own child at home safe, and she knew, working here, how quickly that could change. She guided him to a chair and got him some water. When he drank some water and had rested a minute, she asked what had happened. She knew about the disaster at the field already for she had been taking care of the children as they arrived. This boy needed to tell her what happened for his sake. She had only a minute to give, but she knew that just as much as the children that were bleeding, this one was in shock of another kind. Sometimes the shock of the mind could be far worse then the shock of the body. She held his hand as he recounted the story. He was concerned about his brother and she assured him she would check on him. She had to leave him to go back to work, but she would keep an eye on him. She went in the room where the doctors were working on Reeny. "How is this one Doctor? He looks pretty serious," asked the nurse. The doctor looked up and motioned them out into the hall. "He has some head injury and he has lost his front teeth. He has a fractured arm too. We will fix his arm tonight. The teeth will wait until we see how the head injury mends. Ann, you seem concerned about this one, do you know him?" asked the doctor.

"His brother is in the waiting room, he appears to have run the whole way here from the field. These kids in the Ameriland School don't have their parents here, I just..."

"I know. You want to be all their mothers. You can't, and you look tired. Go home."

"I can't leave that boy out there. Who will contact the parents?"

"Let one of the other nurses do it, you need to go and get some rest."

"No, I want to help this boy, I think we will both get on the space com and contact his family."

"If that is what you want, but this is the tough part."

"I know."

They walked over to Max, and the doctor introduced himself and tried to explain to a fourteen-year-old what was ahead. Max heard nothing past head injury.

"Would you like to go to the space phone with us to talk to your parents?" Nurse Ann asked.

The doctor looked at her quizzically, knowing this might not be a good idea. He trusted Ann's judgment and let her call the shots on this. They walked to the com phone, pressed the numbers and waited. It took a little while. A few minutes later Max was looking at the face of his mother, she looked like she had just arrived home from school.

"Max, is there something wrong?" She did not have to ask. She knew something was seriously wrong.

"Hi, Mrs. Gallagher. First I want to assure you everything will be fine. We have Reeny here with some injuries he sustained in a fall." The doctor spoke up and had his hand on Max's shoulder.

"What happened to Reeny?" Kay looked stricken.

"Mom it will be all right," Max said not wanting to see his mom look so helpless.

"Mrs. Gallagher. I'm Nurse Ann Beal and I know this is a stressful call, but Reeny will be fine. His head injury is minor and he needs to be watched a while."

"Yes Mrs. Gallagher, head injuries like this usually turn out fine as long as he is quiet for a few hours. We will keep him here a couple of days. We are setting a fractured arm and uh some teeth were involved," the doctor continued.

"What happened to his teeth?" Kay's mind raced to the beautiful smile and great big white teeth that occupied Reeny's mouth.

"He lost his front teeth, but you know teeth are easy to replace. This will happen within the next week probably. We will call in a specialist. He will get the best treatment. I would say this boy was blessed to come out with just this amount of injury," the doctor said.

"Max, what happened?" Kay turned to Max.

"They were racing Kaltos. The Kaltos got out of control somehow and everyone was thrown," Max said. He felt so much better talking to his mom and seeing her face.

"Mrs. Gallagher, would you like to continue to talk to Max a while. We will get back to work. We can keep in contact with anything new about Reeny. Head injuries can be tricky, but Reeny is young and he should bounce back quickly enough," the doctor said.

"Yes doctor that is fine. Thank you for the phone call and for taking the time to explain. Thank you Nurse for being with Max right now." Kay could sense that these two took more time than they needed to, judging by the flurry of activity behind them.

As the two walked away Nurse Ann looked at the doctor.

"That is an expensive call for the hospital. Thank you for letting them talk a while longer," Ann said.

"I always think about what it would feel like to be so far from your children. What a sacrifice! I have the feeling these kids are important to all our futures. They are bright and certainly find many new ways to entertain themselves." He was thinking of this night in particular.

Max continued to talk to his mom a few more minutes. His dad was out of town and due back that evening. Luke chimed in at one point and asked what had happened. Kay would deal with explaining things to Luke later. She decided to wait to tell Vince when he arrived home. It would serve no purpose to call on his personal phone. She was upset and wanted to calm down. Max said his good-byes and promised to call when his turn came. Max had missed a call to his parents the week before. Kay made sure to tell him not to miss making the weekly calls. Reeny always called and gave her news of Max.

Max went to check once more on Reeny before he left. Nurse Ann saw him about to leave and slipped a paper in his hand. "If you need me, you call me. This is my number at home. Call anytime, I won't mind," she said and gave him a hug. He felt like he might cry and he wanted to leave quickly. "Thank you." And with that he walked out of the hospital. He was walking in a quieter world than it had been coming in. The air was misty, as it always was at night on Ameriland. It never really rained, and there were two suns so that it was never completely dark even when their moon wasn't full. When the moon was bright on Ameriland, there was nothing as beautiful as this on Earth. Max wasn't enjoying the beauty at the moment, but it wasn't lost on him completely either. He understood Reeny's love for this planet. Max prayed, thanking God for protecting Reeny from fatal injuries. His chest felt swelled and the lump in his throat got bigger as he felt God's presence so vividly at that moment. Max fell to his knees beside the canal and wept. He was alone with his God and he could let himself give in to the tension that had been building. It wasn't just about that night, it was about his life and growing up.

Reeny awoke groggy and confused some hours later. One of the nurses was monitoring the room and realized Reeny was awake. She beeped the doctor on call and she proceeded into the room. Reeny was pulling at the bandages on his face.

"No you don't young man! We worked too hard on you to let you rip all this off," the nurse said as she gently guided his hands away from his face.

"What happened?" Reeny asked, with a voice that sounded like he had cotton in his mouth.

"Do you remember anything?" asked the nurse.

"I think uh maybe. I was at the field racing..." He stopped talking for a second because reality set in, and again the event played over in his brain. He moaned as he relived the moment and the harsh pain he felt. Just then the doctor walked in. "Well didn't expect you to come around so soon. Nice to see you son." With that he stuck his hand out to Reeny. Reeny limply raised his hand and the doctor grasped it with understanding. Reeny's eyes were full of questions and he intended to put this boy at ease.

"Reeny you're going to be all right, don't worry. We have been in touch with your mom and she's reassured we are taking good care of you. Your brother has been here and he talked to your mom. We will let you talk to your parents when you are a little further along. Do you feel all right now?" Reeny nodded, glad the doctor had talked to his mom. He worried about her when she had to hear bad news. She always wanted to fix things and make things better right away.

"Good, now for the news. You have lost a few teeth and suffered a minor head injury. You have a fractured arm, but we can mend that quickly enough. The teeth can be replaced. With the material they use now you won't be able to tell them from your real ones. The head will only improve. I think you will be out of here soon enough. You have been watched over son, I hope you don't try racing Kaltos anymore."

"I may wait awhile on that," replied Reeny.

The doctor turned to the nurse and gave her some instructions. He gave a nod and wave to Reeny as he left the room. The nurse chatted on about some current events as she fluffed his pillow, but he did not comprehend any of it. He was thinking of his parents and longing to be out of this place. They all seemed nice enough, but this was a bummer. He wondered what had happened to the other racers. He turned to the nurse.

"How are the others that were racing that night?"

"Oh mostly cuts and bruises, you all were lucky, I should say." He just had noticed she spoke with an English accent.

"You are from England on Earth aren't you?

"Born and raised. You are from America I can tell. What part?

"Georgia. This is my third year at the Ameriland School."

"I ventured here about five years ago, when they were so desperate for nurses. Pay has been good and it certainly is a good place to live. I didn't have many people back home. Lost my parents to a fire when I was little. They were in the hospital for a long time before they died. That is what made me want to be a nurse, being, you know, at the hospital and all for so long. The nurses became my family so to speak. Oh my, I've got to get on with my shift. I'll be back to talk to ye later." With that she flitted out the door. Reeny was left to contemplate the conversation. He put his head back on the pillow and thought about how good he did have it. He decided not to feel sorry for himself again, and if he did start to, he would think of this nurse. He fell asleep with a prayer going up and thoughts of family, friends, and especially the new friend he had just met.

Kay had decided to take a warm bubble bath that evening before Vince arrived home. He would fly in and take a hover taxi home. He had been in Italy a week and she was glad this was the night he was coming in since she had to give him news of Reeny. She knew she had to calm down and be thankful all would turn out well. Kay hated it that Reeny would be alone tonight, but prayed for God to send a comforter. She had not known He had already taken care of that. While the water was running, she held her hand under it and was deep in thought. A bump against the house aroused her out of the quiet moment. She shrugged her shoulders and went back to her thoughts. It happened again, this time it was louder with each consistent bump. She finally got dressed and went down to see what was going on. Luke and a neighbor were rolling a basketball off the house and catching it. She knew Vince did not like that game, so she yelled out the door to Luke. "Luke you know your dad doesn't like that, just because he is not here doesn't mean you can do that either. Don't you have homework?"

"Oh Mom, you're always spoiling a good time. The homework will be easy. I can do it in no time flat."

"Get inside now and get to work," Kay said firmly. She was in no mood to argue.
Luke looked at his friend and flipped the ball back to him. "See ya later." He walked into the house with an attitude. Kay shook her head and headed back upstairs to the bath. When she finally sunk her body into that warm sudsy bath, she began to relax. A few minutes later she thought she heard more noises, but chalked it up to Luke again. She stayed as long as she dared to, considering she needed to prepare something for Vince to eat. She also wanted to tidy up a bit. As she was walking toward the kitchen, she heard Vince's voice. It was not a tone she liked and she wondered what he was doing home already.

"Kay there you are, where have you been? You have touched the computer again." Kay knew what he meant by this statement. "Touched" was the word he used for anything that was out of whack in the house.

"I always 'touch' the computer," Kay said.

"You know what I mean, like what weird thing did you do? All my documents have been either sent into cyber space or they are misfiled."

"Hi, I'm glad to see you again too," Kay said with a hurt angry voice.

Vince looked up from the computer and realized how bad he had just been.

"I'm sorry honey, of course I'm glad to see you." He walked over to give her a hug.
She wasn't going to give in that quickly. Kay pulled away with a hurt look on her face.

"Honey look, I had to come home and get this settled in the computer and space mailed back to Italy before 7:00. It is real close to that time now, do you have any idea what happened?" Vince asked.

"Why do you think I had anything to do with it? You are always accusing me of messing up something electronic when I 'touch' it. You know, right now that is not important," Kay shot back.

"What do you mean? What do you think I've been doing for a week, playing dominos? Kay this is a very important document and part of this work." Vince was fooling with the computer, but sobs coming from Kay got his attention.

"What is the matter Kay?"

"It is Reeny, he has been hurt. I did not want to tell you like this."

Vince shot out of the chair and grabbed Kay.

"Honey, why didn't you say something? What has happened? Is he all right? What?" Vince hugged her and kissed her face. He brushed the hair from her cheek and looked at her with his deep blue eyes. Kay collected herself and answered his questions.

"Ok so we need to call tonight? Oh Kay, I am so sorry that you had to be alone with this, and then I come home and act like a bear." Vince was hugging her close and tightly.

Kay looked at the time. "Vince the document, it is almost 7:00."

"You were right, that is not important now. I will smooth things over with the engineers tomorrow. Do you know how to get in touch with this hospital? Do you know the com number?" Vince asked.

"Yes, they said they would call. I talked to Max a little and got the number from him. I thought I would go ahead and call."

Kay made the call to the hospital and the kind doctor put their minds at ease. He told them Reeny was awake and seemed to be himself. They wanted to go to him, but the doctor told them by the time they could get there, Reeny would be jumping hurdles.

"Well once again our boys have kept the angels busy," Vince said when they got off the computer phone.

"Would you like something to eat? I can order something up." Kay went toward the kitchen, but Vince caught her arm.

"I ate something on the plane. I want to talk to you for a while."

"Oh I don't know, I might have 'touched' all the electrical things and messed up the home computer system. Are you sure you want to talk to me? Kay asked playfully.

"I said I was sorry. Come on, I was thinking of trying to get to Ameriland in a few months and thought you would like to hear the details," Vince said in a sly voice knowing this would be Kay's dream. When he saw her face, he knew he was forgiven, at least for a while. Vince told her of an opportunity at work that would send him to Ameriland. Things had to be hashed out, but he thought there was a good chance that he would be chosen to go. He told her they would all go if he got the trip. Kay was happy that night as they fell into bed exhausted and glad to be together. Kay was still uneasy with not seeing Reeny, but she knew all would be well. She said her prayers before she slept and trusted her loved ones to God.

When they awoke the next morning they knew it would be a good time to call and talk to Reeny. Kay's heart sank at the sight of her handsome boy's face. All his front teeth were missing. They had put the com phone in his room for the call and he was sitting up in bed.

"Hey Mom, I think I won that Kalto race. It was a big event. You should have seen me," said Reeny and he grinned toothless. Max walked into the room at that time.

"Yeah, who came out better, you or the Kalto? Max went over and punched his brother's arm. Reeny winced.

"Be careful of your brother Max. Don't be hitting on him now," Kay said reaching out to the computer as if to touch her sons.

"Oh, I could take him on and beat him to the ground even in my condition," Reeny said.

"I'd like to see you try!" Max replied. They talked a little longer and Nurse Ann walked into the room.

"I think Reeny needs his medication and rest," she said. They pulled the computer phone out of the room. The doctor came out to the com phone and once again told them Reeny would be fine in a few days. Kay asked again about the mouth and teeth, worried that

171

he would not have his beautiful smile again. He told her he would have a better set of teeth that nothing could knock out. He said the way Reeny lived he would need heavy duty bones and teeth. They all agreed with that. Max talked a few more minutes, and even Luke got up to talk. They didn't talk long before they were teasing each other. They finally said their good-byes and signed off.

A few days later Reeny was back at the dorm. There were letters and cards waiting for him, but he only saw one. His heart beat faster as he picked up the big multicolored card. Karu had made him a card and made up a verse. She could make anyone feel good, and she had a flair for writing. She was very artistic and painted quite a bit. He placed the card under his pillow and read the rest of the cards. The computer phone rang and he turned on the monitor. There was Scouts happy face looking at him.

"Hey toothless wonder, I heard they gave you the award for winning the Kalto race. Hope it was worth it," Scout said laughing; but when she saw Reeny's face she almost wanted to cry. She maintained her good nature though Reeny saw the slight worried expression she let slip for a moment.

"Scout, I'll be back to myself in no time and we will play virtual tennis again soon. I know I can beat you next time," Reeny said.

"Face it, I'm the champ," Scout said.

"Have you talked to Karu?"

"I knew that was coming. She wanted to run to your side the minute it happened. It was too dangerous to get out on the field. She has been so worried and she has called the hospital every day. They were only letting family calls through. Too many Ameriland students were trying to call. We will call you from this room then. It is better that way. They monitor all calls at her home. She is still afraid of taking that chance. Her parents almost always make her go home on the weekends. That is why she is home on Saturdays. They must suspect something," Scout explained.

"I understand," Reeny said. He was happy to know she had cared so much.

"Look, as soon as you are all patched up, we will take another trip to Karu's house," Scout said.

"Sure I would like that. It will be a few weeks before I can go too far. I will be taking classes through the computer for a while. A nurse will be checking on me every day. I kind of miss Mom," Reeny said and realized he may have opened the door for a joke from Scout.

"Reeny, from what I could tell about your mom, she would be here if she could fold space somehow," Scout said.

"Yes, I hate it when she gets worried. I knew when I talked to her she wanted to be right here taking care of me," Reeny said in a sad voice.

"Well I have to go to a class. I'll call you tomorrow. Talking to Karu may cheer you up," Scout said in a hurry, realizing the time had gotten away from her. She said good-bye quickly and her face faded from the screen. Reeny was left alone to contemplate things. Jon was in class and he would not see him until later. He wasn't going to do class work for a couple of days, so he turned to his virtual hand held games. He also was thinking of what to say to Karu, and he smiled to himself.

Max went to spend time with Reeny on his first day back to his dorm. He had classes to attend in the morning, but came as soon as he could. It would be a week tomorrow since the accident. He had plans to meet Summer Faye at the park for lunch on Saturday. Max was a little uneasy about going to the park right now, the memory of that night was raw in his mind. He tried to help Reeny a little with things and Jon came in and took over. Max knew Jon would be there for Reeny and take good care of him, so he said his good-byes and went back to his room.

The next day he met Summer Faye at the spot they had met before. He looked down at the few grazing Kaltos, they were slowly moving to their own time. That horrible evening seemed like it had happened a long time ago, but at the same time played in his mind like it had just happened. He could not explain this. Summer Faye was speaking to him and he turned around.

"What?" Max asked.

"Wow you were gone. I know it was pretty bad to see your brother in that accident last week. Are you all right?" Summer Faye asked concerned.

"Oh sure, it's just that, you know, I can't seem to forget. It's weird, it is like a bad dream."

"You really saved your brother's life. You pulled him out of that stampede. Does he know?"

"I don't think he remembers much about that night and he doesn't talk about it much," replied Max.

"We heard rumors they arrested Kel and Adu," Summer Faye said.

"Kel and Adu, those scabs, what did they do?" Max asked.

"They think they caused the Kalto stampede. They found a rope around the female Kalto that was on the field and knew someone had done the dirty trick. It seems Kel has a big mouth and bragged about it," Summer Faye said.

"Oh, if I could get my hands on those two. They are always hanging around the school and making trouble!" Max said angrily.

"I don't think they will hang around anywhere anytime soon," Summer Faye replied.

"I guess not. I wonder what they will do to them?" Max wondered.

"I don't know, but I wouldn't want to be in their shoes." Summer Faye shook her head.

They continued to talk and eat. They had a good time and left for the dorms. Max was happy about things. He was glad Reeny would recover and that Summer Faye liked him. He was going to have a hard time forgiving those two scoundrels. He would have to pray for help with that. His parents had taught him about forgiveness, but he had never experienced this much anger at other people. He wondered how someone could be so mean and careless. Max would go to sleep that night talking to God about these very thoughts.

Chapter 14

Rumors of war were still being spread. The Talcots of Russo wanted part of Ameriland, the part they had first settled years ago. Most of the Talcots had moved back to Russo after it proved not to be too lucrative on Ameriland. America had eventually taken most of the planet as colonies. Since then there had been discoveries of many important minerals in the former Talcot territory. The Talcots recently were experiencing unrest and warring, as they have for years with the other Russo's. They felt they were not getting their fair share of jobs and positions due to their odd appearance. Talcots were the only ones on Russo with the third eye. They were easy to spot and prejudices did abound, just as every culture has. Right or wrong the Talcots were boiling, and in a matter of time that pot would boil over and Ameriland would be where the pot spilled. They wanted that land back, and they wanted off a planet they considered hostile to them.

Word went to Washington and all world leaders. Intelligence agents had been warning the government for years that something like this might occur. The government began to look into the new war ships and give them more priority. So far Ameriland had a Lockheed branch near the Ameriland School, making experimental ships. More contracts were going to be thrown that way quickly and with that, employment would have to match the demand.

Vince had been in meetings all day and Kay had tried to call him. The holiday season was approaching rapidly and Kay was always calling Vince at this busy time, but she had not reached him on this particular day. Vince was late coming in. He had an odd look on his face when he came in the door.

"What's the matter honey, have a bad day? I tried to call several times. We were asked to dinner on Thursday evening and I wanted to check with you. You know Fred and Nancy, they always invite us over near the holidays." Kay was chopping onions and talking at the same time. She finally looked up and saw the expression on his face. Something was up. She went over and kissed his cheek and questioned him again.

"Kay, I don't know how to say this. I have good news and bad news." Vince was torn as to how to tell Kay his news.

"Vince go ahead and give the bad news."

"There is talk that the Talcots may go to war," Vince said.

"They have been in a war of some kind for decades with the rest of Russo," Kay replied puzzled that this was any news.

"No, I mean there is reason to believe they will try to get their land back on Ameriland."

"Rumors have flown around for years about that too. Vince do you know something?" Kay asked.

"Yes, that is where I was today. We had meetings all day. They want me to go to our Lockheed branch on Ameriland to be on the ground floor for these new ships they are assembling," Vince said.

"For how long?" Kay's mind was turning this over.

"They want us to relocate to Ameriland."

"You mean us? We are going to move to Ameriland?" Kay was trying to contain her emotions. She knew what Vince meant by good and bad news. She would be with her boys, but if there was going to be a war, she would have brought her boys home. Now it seemed they were all going to be in the middle of it. She did not know how to respond to this information.

"I know what you're thinking. The territory in dispute is not anywhere near Lockheed or the school," Vince said quickly. Luke walked into the room at that time and they ceased to talk.

"What's up dad?" Luke said taking his music plugs out of his ears.

"Not much, what's up with you?" Vince asked back.

"You don't want to know, believe me," Kay said.

"What happened today? Vince asked.

"It wasn't my fault," Luke said as he grabbed a banana and went quickly back to his room. Vince looked at Kay with a questioning face. Kay shook her head, as if to say, "don't ask." They continued to talk into the night about the plans. Kay was excited about being with her boys all the time, but the nagging worry of war was ahead of all her thoughts. They prayed to make the right decisions that night before falling to sleep.

The news reports were hinting at the unrest on Russo, but not much information was available for the public. So far the politics of Russo stayed on Russo. The Russo's on Ameriland tried to stay away from the disputes in their homeland. They considered Ameriland their home. There were a few who spoke out and caused problems. Talcots were the most restless. They were looking pretty bad, as a race of people, to the rest of the planets. Some of them were concerned for their safety outside and apart from their own fellow beings.

Chapter 15

Reeny had fully recovered from his injuries and decided to take Pubcan down to the city. There was a teen club that was popular and it was a safe place to be. Jon had some project to work on and declined the invitation to go. Scout said she was going and would try to get Karu to go. Karu's parents seldom let her go out at night, so it would be a long shot if she showed up. Reeny seldom went to the clubs, he usually found them lame, but for the chance to see Karu he would go anywhere. It was Friday night and nothing else was going on, so he was on his way. He got on the nearest Pubcan boat and settled in the seat facing the water. He had to admit to himself that this was a beautiful ride by any standards. The boat had floated awhile when Reeny looked around on the boat to see who might be aboard he knew. Uno was sitting in the back looking rather lonely, so Reeny went back to speak to him.

"Hey Uno, what's up?" Reeny said and gave Uno a slight slap on the shoulder. Uno was startled out of his deep thoughts, but gave Reeny a quick smile and a wink with his third eye.

"Reeny, my favorite trouble maker. Come sit down," Uno said and moved over and motioned to the seat. Reeny sat down and he couldn't help but notice the troubled look on Uno's face, even though he tried to hide it.

"You must be getting ready for the celebration of Christmas. Do you miss your parent's at this time of the year? Uno asked.

"Yes I do. Mom and Dad said they were going to have good news to tell us in a few days. They were working on the details. My bet is Dad's finally come up with a trip here for the holidays. Mom's been wanting to visit here for a long time," Reeny said.

"Well Reeny that would be so nice. I wish my parents were still alive. You know I have two grown kids on Russo. I don't see them much. Their mom left after a year here. She couldn't stand to be away from home. I was too young and stupid to stop her. I always thought that if I made a good living here she would return to me. It never happened and time just slipped by. Now I worry about the warring going on. Oh there have always been spats between our people, but not like now. I just wonder what is going to happen. I am concerned about my family," Uno said sadly.

"Uno, do you think it is that bad?" Reeny asked.

"I think so this time."

"What would you do if war broke out? Would you go back home, or try to get your family here?"

"I don't think it will be long before Ameriland will be pulled into this one," Uno said.

"Do you know something?" Reeny asked anxiously.

"There has always been talk of returning to the Cavhill territory. The land looks so much like Russo. That is why they settled that region so many centuries ago. The Talcots are always looking for somewhere to feel safe. I don't go along with the radical Talcots, they get too greedy and pushy. I think we Talcots always feel like outsiders and that is the reason to look to Ameriland. Talcots feel like Cavhill could be that promised land," Uno said as he looked across the water.

"How do you feel about it?" Reeny asked.

"I don't know. What would I do if the Talcots went to war for Cavhill? What loyalty do I share and where do I belong?" Uno asked, and Reeny could see all three eyes tearing up. "Perhaps I should not worry so right now," Uno quickly said seeing the concern on his young friend's face.

"Uno, I hope to never be on a different side than you." With that Reeny put his hand on Uno's shoulder and Uno patted Reeny's hand. Uno was unable to say anything and he bit back the tears.

Reeny left Uno at the next stop. He went toward the club on foot instead of by shuttle. He always liked to think about things and be alone. This was a good time to walk and think. What if war came? What would he do? He thought about the possibility of his parents coming to Ameriland and that made him happier. He could show Mom so many things. He could see her face now, and Dad would love to see the flight school. Luke would bounce around happily. Yes, those thoughts were much easier on the mind than the other thought of war.

Scout met him at the door and he could see from her look that she had no success at getting Karu there.

"Where have you been?" Scout asked.

"I don't know. I was just messing around. Karu's not here is she?"

"No," Scout said.

"I didn't get my hopes up too much. Who's here?" Reeny asked.

"Not too many people tonight. Hannah is here, I think she thought Jon would come."

"I thought he told her he had this project due."

"He did, she just thought he might come for a while," Scout said looking toward the door. "Well are you coming in?" She turned back to ask Reeny.

Reeny left the club within an hour, and even though it never really gets dark on Ameriland, the streets were lit up for Christmas. Amerilanders celebrated Christmas just the same as Earth since the Christian faith dominated the planet. Amerilanders had other celebrations that were different from Earth's, but Christmas stayed the same. Reeny was thankful to hear the Christmas carols sounding out of the stores and he walked peacefully along. Hovercrafts passed at high speeds and the mist of the night settled around him. He started to form a plan. He would love to zip around in a hovercraft. Maybe if he got a job somewhere, he could afford an old one. He was pretty sure he would see his parents soon and he would talk to his dad about it. Mom wouldn't be too thrilled, but she would come around. He looked up to see a "Now Hiring" sign over the pizza shop, and before he knew it his feet stepped inside. He talked to the owner and got an application. The pay sounded good and he could start right away, with the permission of the school. One had to have good grades to take on a job from the Ameriland School. Reeny wasn't concerned because he was pulling his grades up in hopes of getting to flight school. He now had more reason to get to flight school. He wanted to fly those new birds. He raced home to find his com had a message. It was from his parents, they would call back later. Max came into the room. "Mom and Dad left a message for me to come here so they could talk to us. What's up?" Max asked.

"My guess is they will come here for a visit soon. Maybe they are coming at Christmas. It will be in three weeks. They can take the new route and be here on time," Reeny answered.

"Do you really think Dad is going to take that much time off of work?" Max asked.

"Maybe, you know how Mom's been lately."

"Well, I'll have to hear this with my own ears. Have you talked to Karu lately?" Max asked, changing the subject.

"Yes, I talked to her from her room when Scout put in her code. If Karu puts her code in the computer calling system, her parents will find out. They look at the printout of calls at the end of the month. She goes home almost every weekend, so I can't see her like I used to. I used to sneak over. Scout thinks her parents suspect something," Reeny said.

"They probably know something is up. That's too bad. I'm sort of dating Summer Faye," Max said boldly.

"Yeah, I've seen her around. She is cute."

Max smiled, and about that time the com phone rang. They raced to the monitor pushing each other, and one of them pushed the "on" button. Their mom and dad appeared on the screen. They were both grinning.

"Are you coming for a visit?" Max asked and Reeny kicked him on the foot.

"Ouch!" Max yelled.

"What is the matter son?" Kay asked.

"Oh, nothing. What is your news?" Max asked.

"Max, you are partly right. We are coming to Ameriland." Vince decided to let that news digest for a moment before giving out the rest of the news.

"Great, will you be here for Christmas?" Reeny quickly asked.

"No, we won't be ready in time for Christmas. You see son we are moving to Ameriland. Lockheed has a position for me there. We won't make it until February," Vince replied.

"What do you think boys?" Kay's hands were clasped together as she looked at her boys' faces. Her face was radiant. The boys both noticed their mom's excitement. They were still at a loss for words. They had not expected anything like this.

"Hey dumb and dumber, can't you talk?" That was Luke chiming in behind his parent's.

"Honey, be kind to your brothers," Kay said.

"Hey, if what they say is true little brother, you better start worrying. You don't stand a chance against the two of us," Reeny said.

"Yeah, you will be our punching bag soon," Max said and he was throwing punches in the air, as if to make a point. Luke looked wide-eyed and gulped.

Vince and Kay went over the details with the boys before signing off. They were all excited about the turn of events. Max and Reeny stayed up late discussing what this would mean to them.

Reeny told Max of his plan to purchase a hovercraft of his own. Max was excited. He thought that if his brother had a craft it might offer him some freedom too. They both decided to wait a while before discussing it with the parents. Dad might be all right with it, but Mom would worry. They had mixed feelings about the move to Ameriland. The thought occurred to them that they might not see Earth for a very long time once their parents and Luke arrived.

"It is going to be so hard to leave my parents," Kay said one evening when things calmed down around them. Vince had just walked into the room and his hands were behind his back.

"Honey, I know this is going to be hard on you, but we will try to visit once a year," Vince said.

"It will be expensive." Kay replied.

Vince smiled and brought from behind his back a bunch of roses. Vince had a new hobby. He had started growing roses in a space in the back. They had done well and he often picked some for Kay to put around the house.

"Oh those are pretty. Your new bushes are doing well," Kay said and smiled one of her winning smiles. Vince always liked Kay's smile.

"I worked up a package deal at Lockheed. One trip a year, paid for, if I locate to Ameriland. They accepted the deal. I did not say anything to you about it until I found out if they would go for it," Vince said.

"That makes me feel better. I'll call Mom, she has fretted about this. She is happy and all, but I can tell that she is worried. The older they get, the more worried they get about us being away from them. Being farther away is one thing and being on another planet is something else," Kay said as she went to the phone.

Time flew as preparations were made to move to Ameriland. So many new and exciting things would be happening. For Kay who had never really traveled much throughout her life, this was a strange new beginning. What motivated her most was the need to be close to her children. Kay would probably walk through fire for her children and this had not been a difficult decision for her. She had gotten the feeling that Reeny felt more at home on Ameriland then he did on Earth. In her heart she knew he would settle on Ameriland, even when he got out of school. He would probably apply for flight school as soon as he could after graduation and that would be another four years or so in flight school. He took school a lot more seriously now. Kay now worried about her parents.

She had a brother and sister with families close by. Her mom and dad would have plenty of family, but when the circle is broken, life is not the same. This would be a new experience for all of the family because they had remained so close.

Christmas was upon them before long and the hectic days of the holiday kept them all busy. Thanksgiving had flown by so fast that it was hardly noticed. The family had all gathered around a space com to talk to Reeny and Max on Thanksgiving. They were doing well and Reeny had his old smile back. Kay was the only one who noticed a slight lisp to his voice since the accident. Only a mom would have known. When Kay mentioned it to Vince, he told her it was in her imagination. She knew that the operation on his mouth had altered his speech, but she let it go. She had to let go of a lot of things she worried about and leave it to God.

Chapter 16

The New Year brought in new hope. Washington was still getting reports of unrest among the Talcots. Ameriland became a little worried and tried to brace for the worst. Hopefully some peace talks could end the strife and some solution could be made to calm the waters.

Reeny had gradually become a better student as he became more serious about flight school. Reeny was the type of person to have to see the reason to do things. He took nothing on the surface and questioned everything. If it made sense enough to pursue, he gave it his all. Reeny had a reason to pursue being the best at school because he had a goal. He still wanted to get into flight school a year earlier than most and he was working at being there next year. He wanted a job to buy things and to feel independent. When he got the pizza job, he was thrilled and set out to be the best pizza worker.

Reeny went to work each evening at the pizza parlor. He saw East side Canots and Talcots not to mention all the nationalities of

America. Reeny had the ability to get along with anyone and enjoyed the light bantering with the customers. When he got home, he could not even explain it to himself, but he loved the tired feeling that a good day at work brings. Reeny was happy moving about, and learning was easy at school, so this was the outlet he found that kept him out of trouble.

One evening while he was waiting on the tables, he noticed two Talcots staring at him and making comments. He ignored them, because he knew they were on the radical side of things. Since talk of the war and the Talcots reclaiming some of Ameriland, all the radicals were causing trouble. They were always marching in the streets and doing other things to cause trouble. It was a big part of the news these days. Reeny continued to work.

"Hey Reeny, what is up man." Some students from Ameriland had arrived at the shop. He greeted them and they sat down. He took their order and started back to the kitchen and one of the Talcots tripped him. He stumbled, and when he reclaimed his footing he gave the Talcots a hard look.

"It looks like this little human from that frilly school can't even walk," said the Talcot who tripped him. They all had a big laugh.

Reeny turned red more with anger than embarrassment and walked on into the kitchen. The owner noticed the exchange and also noticed Reeny had kept his calm. The other students did not take the slight to the school very well and words were exchanged. Things started to get out of hand and Joe, the owner, asked all of them to leave. They left still flinging words at each other.

"Reeny thanks for keeping your cool with those Talcots," Joe said to Reeny as he got ready to close down for the evening. Reeny was sweeping and just nodded. His pride had been hurt a little, but he would survive.

"You are a good worker, maybe you can manage soon. You are management material. You would be able to make more money," Joe was saying as Reeny prepared to leave.

"I don't know Joe, I can't put in any more hours," Reeny replied.

"You would not have to. I need someone in the evening to manage. I want to spend more time at home and I need someone I can trust here," Joe said.

"Well I'll think about it," Reeny said as he tiredly went out the door. He said good night to some of the patrons still outside lingering. He took a short cut through the alleyway, like he always did, but felt apprehensive as he entered the dark place. He heard something behind him and the trash cans fell over as a Sequata screeched and fled the other way. Reeny shook his head and continued. He thought he saw a shadow and chided himself for being a scary cat. He walked at a much faster pace until the shadows were real and standing in front of him. It was the trouble-making Talcots that were in the pizza shop.

"Well, we have the little frilly human boy!" One of them said with a chilling laugh.

"Yeah, I wonder what this piece of human garbage is made of?" another one said.

Reeny was looking at three figures and looking into nine eyes. It was not a position he wished to be in. He prayed real hard to get out of this in one piece.

"Hey, you guys don't want to cause trouble. I mean, messing with Ameriland students can get you into big trouble," Reeny said.

"Well you are not on Ameriland school property and I believe that is where your protection is. Little boy I think you are the one in trouble." And with that he grabbed Reeny and held him while another hit him in the stomach. Reeny bent over and gasped. They kicked him again, but before another punch could be thrown they started running.

Reeny looked up to see why they ran and saw some shadowy figures coming toward him. It was Uno and some of his friends. He picked Reeny up and helped him back to the shop. Joe saw them coming and opened the door.

"What happened? Did those Talcots get you? I thought they left too easily," Joe was asking.

"I think he is all right. Maybe he will need some ice for his face. Those Talcots must have been waiting for him. I saw him go down in the alley and tried to catch up with him. I thought we could catch the Pubcan with him. When we rounded the corner, we saw the commotion in the alley. When they saw us coming they fled fast enough," Uno said.

Reeny refused to get treatment at the hospital. He had had enough of hospitals for a while. He seemed to feel fine on the ride back on the Pubcan. Uno and his friends occupied him on the ride.

"You are going to have a whale of a headache and a good shiner on that eye." Uno finally broke the silence of the foursome.

"I'll be fine. I just don't want Mom to find out right now. They don't know I have this job," Reeny said.

"Why did you take a job, most Ameriland students find school too intense to work?" Uno asked.

"It makes me feel like I'm doing something for myself and earning money for me. Besides, I want a craft to ride around in," Reeny replied.

"Oh I see, you want your freedom. Maybe it is not time for that. We would like to keep you alive until you get to adulthood," Uno said.

"I want to keep my job. Please don't let the school know what happened. They will investigate and probably decide not to let me work. I had to show them I could do this and keep my grades up in order to have this job," Reeny pleaded.

"That is against what I should do, Reeny. I feel the school should know. I'll keep quiet for now, but anything else has to be reported. I know they just wanted to scare you because they would have hit you a lot harder. I don't think they would have done anything more then a roughing up, but it concerns me." Uno shook his head as he spoke. He did not feel comfortable with this situation. He knew Reeny was right. The school would take his job away from him. They would have no choice. The safety of the students came first. He hoped this was an isolated incident.

"Hey, I have an old craft that I don't use anymore. I never cared for them. A little fixing up would get it going. You could buy it for a few credits," Baco spoke up and they all turned his way.

"Reeny, maybe you should consider getting this old craft off Baco's hands until you can get something better. That would give you more safety to and from work. I'm sure Joe would let you park it in front. You would not be on the streets at night," Uno said. He wanted Reeny to be safe and this would give him a degree of safety.

"I'll have a look at it. It might be something I could use for a while." Reeny had perked up and was feeling better about things.

The next morning Reeny went to look at the craft that Baco had. He felt he could fix it up with the money he had earned so far. The deal was done and he sputtered and spat down the hovercraft lanes until he got back to the school. When he came to a stop it just fell out of mid-air rather then glide to a nice landing. The crafts usually hovered around a foot off the ground, this one hovered only about eight inches. When the dust settled from the abrupt landing, Reeny saw some of his fellow students hanging outside watching him. The craft gave one final big steamy sigh as it was turned off.

"Reeny, what did you drag in this time? Looks like a piece of junk." His friends were yelling comments about the craft and laughing. Reeny was used to his ideas being laughed at, so he never cared. This was a means to an end for him, and he intended to make the most of it. Hoverability could mean a lot of freedom and that was worth it.

Reeny was called into Mr. Stockwell's office that afternoon. It was a Saturday and Reeny wondered what was up. He hoped he had not heard of the incident the night before.

"Reeny, come in." Mr. Stockwell's door was open when Reeny stepped out of the hallway into the secretary's office. She was not there on Saturdays so Mr. Stockwell had left the office door open.

"You wanted to see me?" Reeny asked nervously.

Mr. Stockwell looked up from his papers and looked into Reeny's face.

"Quite a shiner you have there! Did you have a run-in with someone?" Mr. Stockwell had been told there were words flung at the pizza parlor between the Talcots and some of his students. He now knew it had gone further.

"I ran into a pole. I can be so clumsy sometimes," Reeny replied.

Mr. Stockwell knew Reeny did not have a clumsy bone in his body, but he let it pass.

"Reeny, if this job causes any problems at all, I can't let you keep it," Mr. Stockwell said.

"I know, and I won't let you down. I want to work," Reeny said anxiously. He knew Mr. Stockwell had already figured it out.

"Reeny, you now have brought upon the campus one truly questionable piece of machinery. Can you explain? You of course know crafts are not permitted without proper authorization."

"Well I was going to get permission. I found this deal and couldn't let it pass. Mr. Stockwell, you know sometimes riding the canals at a certain time lately has been dangerous. The radical Tacots have been causing trouble more and more. You see, Mr. Stockwell, I thought the craft would offer more safety. I can park it close to where I need to be and lessen the chances of any unwanted exchanges."

Mr. Stockwell found this argument to be a valid one, considering the current problems his students now faced. He thought this probably was a good solution to Reeny's situation. Times had changed and were likely to get worse before they got better. He was going to have to think of many ways to keep his students safe in an uncertain time. Reeny was a step ahead of his fellow students in his knowledge of the Talcots.

"Reeny, I still need to talk to your parents about this job. I've waited to see just how long you would last. I think you are made of tougher stuff than I gave you credit. I know your parents will be here in the spring. You will probably live with them and you will be under their rules at that time. I hope they let you keep your job and that thing you call a craft. I will speak to them on your behalf."

"Thank you Mr. Stockwell. I will stay out of trouble and you won't regret this."

Reeny went out of the room happy and ready to work on his craft. Mr. Stockwell was left shaking his head. He wondered what would become of Reeny. He had most certainly added color to the school since his arrival. He had often wondered if he would ever conform and make it. Mr. Stockwell was left with the thought that he was glad Reeny did not really conform. He did not know why he felt that way, but for whatever reason, he liked that boy.

Chapter 17

"My parents are dead." The tears were pouring from Luke's eyes as he sat in front of the cyber phone talking to someone unknown.

"Luke, what are you doing?" Kay was putting down some boxes she was packing and found Luke talking on the cyber phone. She looked to see who he was talking to and it was a saleslady.

"Sorry," Kay said to the lady and turned off the monitor.

"Luke, stop telling the salespeople we are dead," Kay said giving Luke a hard look.

"Mom, they are so much fun to mess with," Luke said as he backed out the door. He knew he had gotten on the wrong side of his mom this morning. He backed right into Vince, who was munching on a bagel and had stepped out of the kitchen to see what the commotion was.

"What is going on?" Vince said as he took another bite of bagel.

"Vince, Luke is telling salespeople that we are dead," Kay said, hoping Vince would speak to Luke about his tall tales.

"Good, they will stop calling us," Vince said. Kay just looked at Vince, and Luke laughed and went out the door before anything else could be said.

"Vince how could you encourage him? Now we are on a dead list," Kay said exasperated.

"Dead list? There's a dead list?" Vince asked with an amused look on his face. Kay just shook her head and yelled up the stairs for Luke to keep packing his room.

Packing was coming along well and they were set to leave in a few days. Nerves had been on edge as they are when there is moving involved. Kay had the family over the Saturday before, and it had been very emotional. This was probably the last gathering of them all for a while. Saying good-bye to her fellow teachers had also been hard; church was harder still. Kay had grown up there and the children all were dedicated there. How would she cope with so much change? A prayer for help was never far from her lips as she looked forward to being with her children in an uncertain world.

"Hey, I saw that piece of junk out in the cybercraft parking lot. What did you have to do, pull it here?" Max stuck his head around in Reeny's room as he was talking.

"From what I heard, he almost had to," Jon replied. Reeny was working on a paper and really wasn't interested in what they said or thought.

"What are you working on?" Max asked, surprised Reeny found any school work that took up his time.

"I've started studying for the flight school exam."

"Reeny you have two more years," Max said.

"No wrong. I have until next year."

"How do you figure that?" Max could not believe Reeny could be serious.

"I'm going in early. If I pass this exam with a high score, it can happen." Reeny looked up with a determined look on his face.

Max knew that look, and he knew when Reeny decided something, it was all but done.

"Why?" was all Max could ask.

"Because I don't see any reason why not. I'm going anyway and I want to fly the new space ships," Reeny said in a matter-of-fact way. Jon just looked at Max and shrugged.

Max left to go see Summer Faye. He was giving Reeny's craft some thought. He could get some rides from him. He thought he had better start being nice to him. Maybe he would take Summer Faye to that Pizza place tonight and see Reeny in action. He had heard some rumors about this place and Reeny.

Reeny had managed to get the craft running pretty well and was using it quite a lot. Reeny visited Karu often, sometimes with Scout and sometimes without her. Scout had been right in figuring Reeny would grow on Karu's parents. They thought of him as a friend and knew he was a good person. They could tell he had been brought up godly and felt a certain connection with him, even though they worshiped differently. They would still prefer Karu to date an Amerilander. American blood ran thick in the family, so they would not be surprised if she fell for an American.

War continued to be on the lips of Amerilanders. They could not help but feel the unrest around them. They were suspicious of all Talcots, even though all Talcots did not believe in the radical ideas of those wanting war. In their lifetime, peace had always abounded, now coping with this rumbling volcano had proved more then some could take. Fights broke out often and the patrols were out in force. They hired many new patrols in the city and canals. It certainly looked like a different Ameriland than when Reeny first stepped on this planet.

It was almost spring on Earth. Reeny and Max had talked about how they missed the seasons. It was beautiful all the time on Ameriland. Sometimes one has to see the winter before he can appreciate the hope that spring brings. Reeny often reflected on this. Reeny was a deep thinker and often wondered if that was the way the Amerilanders had been, lost in paradise. They had been at peace in a beautiful place for decades, now they were going to face a winter in their history, not the cold kind, but the kind that comes from hate. On Reeny's young shoulders rested the thought of his parents coming here to a place that could explode. He seemed to be the only one of his peers who worried. He would get sullen at times, because he thought too hard and too deep. Laughter of his fellow comrades rang out around him and echoed in his ears. He could not join this lightheartedness, for he felt he had a job to do and things to accomplish. His drive was overpowering at times and it sometimes isolated those around him.

Reeny was now night manager at the Pizza store. It was tough to keep his grades up and get enough sleep to go on. Fortunately

Reeny had a photographic memory, which allowed him to retain anything that went into that brain of his. His abilities were not lost on the owner of the pizza place, thus the reason at such a young age he was given so much responsibility. Reeny loved the satisfaction work gave him.

"Hey Max, where is Summer Faye tonight?" Reeny asked when Max arrived at the store one evening. The store had become a sort of hangout for the school and Max had come in several times with Summer Faye.

"She is hanging out with some of her girl friends," Max replied.

"Girls do that now and again. I think they gossip and stuff. They do each others hair and all that, you know." Reeny spoke as if he were an expert on girls, but what boy hasn't been dumped on a perfectly good date night by the pull of a pack of girls. It was an uncomfortable position, knowing one might be the subject of conversation among them.

"I was wondering, uh... Reeny." Max started talking and stopped not sure how to ask.

"How much money do you need? Have you been betting on Kalto races again?" Reeny said in a scolding manner.

"Yes, but this is it, no more!" Max said quickly.

"Mom and Dad should be arriving next week. You had better get your act together. You know if Mom finds out, she will ream you good."

"OK, I know. Just this one more payoff and I'm through for good."

"No, you will not get the money, instead you will work it off here." With that Reeny threw him a towel and pointed to a table that needed cleaning.

"Oh man, you got to be kidding. Come on Ren, please." Max was following him back to the kitchen pleading.

"I think a couple of nights here working will get you the money you need. It is this way or none." Reeny turned around.

"Oh all right." With a sigh he looked over at a table of Canots who were sneering at him. He got busy quickly, knowing Reeny meant business. He would give up gambling for sure if he was going to have to work in this hole.

"Are you tired?" Reeny asked as they got into his craft to head back to the school.

"Yes I'm tired. How can you stand that place?" Max replied as he put his head against the back of the chair.

"Well, don't kid yourself, you are going to have to stand it another couple of days."

Reeny looked over and saw that Max seemed dead to the world.

"Mom must be enjoying the trip here. I can see her now, talking Dad into all that stuff on board." Max broke the long silence.

"Yeah, and I can see Dad trying to get out of all that stuff. You know how he analyzes everything until Mom gives up," Reeny said.

"Luke won't let either of them rest until he has done it all, I'm sure," Max was saying as they turned into the school gate.

"Yes, Luke is a little scammer. He knows how to get around Dad, which is amazing. He seems to get away with a lot more than we did."

"Well, I think we can make life more interesting with our little brother here with us," Max jokingly said.

"Yeah, but we can't hurt him too bad. It will be good to have our family together again. I have not had time to think on it much, but Dad said they had a place up in the hills overlooking the canal. The company cyber-spaced information and arrangements were made," Reeny said as he parked the craft and it fell with its usual grace.

"Reeny, man, when are you going to fix the landing gears? I think my back is broken!" Max exclaimed as he rubbed his back.

"You get used to it. I forgot to tell you to hang onto the door handle, that helps lessen the fall. Sorry." Reeny started out of the craft.

"So we are going to live in the hills. That is a nice place to live. Mom will love it," Max said finally after walking a minute to make sure everything was in place.

Reeny made the usual Saturday trip to Karu's the following morning. He pulled up to the yard in front and the craft fell out of the air while kicking up the dust as it landed. When the dust was settling, Scout's face suddenly appeared close to the window. It startled Reeny and he jumped. Scout's laughter rang out.

"What is the matter with you? Are you paranoid?" Scout asked as he embarked from the craft.

"Hey Scout. I thought you weren't coming today. You did not call me to pick you up," Reeny said.

"Are you kidding? I would rather take my chances on Pubcan. This thing can be a hazard to your health, not to mention dangerous," Scout said as she eyed the craft.

"I hear you are studying for the flight exam. Are you taking it this summer when you turn seventeen?" Scout asked as they walked toward the door. Before he could answer, Karu had opened the door and stood there smiling.

They settled with some food next to the pond in the back of Karu's house. The conversation was light with the usual kidding around. Reeny never seemed to be able to talk to Karu alone since her parents insisted that she return home on the weekends. Scout didn't like it because they had had so much fun on the weekends when they were at school. They were not in trouble or anything, it was just that there were many kids to hang out with and do things with. Karu was stuck in the country with no one else to talk to or hang with on the weekends. She found it stifling, but Karu did not complain or give her parents a hard time. If it had been Scout, it would have been a different story.

"Karu, I guess since there is so much talk of war, your parents won't consider ever leaving you at school for the weekend," Scout said.

"Well, I did not want to say anything, but they are considering commuting me everyday. Ross, the driver, would take me daily," Karu said sadly.

"You mean we wouldn't be roommates? Oh Karu, I hope you will speak up for yourself. Try to talk them out of it!" Scout pleaded.

"You would be safer staying at school then commuting. Talcots would be less likely to attack the school. They know America would take quick action," Reeny said.

"I know. I think no one feels safe right now. It is like a boiling pot. At least they are not trying to take me out of the school altogether," Karu said as she reached over and threw some crumbs in the water for the red ducks.

"When are your parents arriving Reeny?" Karu asked after a long silence.

"Next Saturday. I was going to ask if maybe you could come with me to the station. I would like them to meet you," Reeny said with hope that he would get a positive reply.

"Oh Reeny, I would like to go, but I would have to ask Mom and Dad. They might let me," Karu said.

"Well can I go?" Scout asked.

"I thought you did not want to ride in the craft." Reeny gave her a look.

"I can meet you there. Maybe Karu and I could meet you there. Do you think your parents might go for it?" Scout said turning to Karu. Scout knew Karu's parents might not want her riding in Reeny's craft. She was trying to save the day, like Scout always does. Reeny picked up on the whole thing and gave Scout a nod.

"I'll ask. I'll call you next week. I will have to find a good time to ask," Karu replied.

Scout braved the trip home with Reeny in the craft. She wanted to talk to him and this was the best way.

"Look Reeny, about this flight school exam, I've been giving it some thought." Scout started the conversation but Reeny put his hand up.

"Don't try and talk me out of it," Reeny said.

"I wasn't. I will be seventeen in April. I can take the exam too," Scout said turning to Reeny anxiously.

"Scout, I thought you were over it. This is not fun and games," Reeny said.

"Is that what you think I am, fun and games?"

"Well you're not exactly serious about a lot of things, Scout."

"And you don't know me. I thought we could study together."

"Scout, I'm really serious!"

"I am too!"

Reeny saw a determined look on Scouts face and gave in.

"All right, maybe. Jon has decided to give it a chance too."

"Oh this will be..." Scout started to say more but stopped.

"Don't you dare say fun," Reeny scolded.

"I was going to say intense," Scout lied, but Reeny knew her too well.

"Hold onto the handle quickly!" Reeny exclaimed.

"What?" Scout asked, but did what she was told.

The craft fell in the parking space and Scout was still hanging on the door handle.

"Let me check my bones to see if any are broke," Scout said as she patted her body and fixed her hair.

"I can take you over to your school, if you like," Reeny said.

"No thank you, no... uh I think I'll take Pubcan across. I want to arrive in one piece." With that Scout gathered herself together and scooted toward the canal with a wave good-bye.

Chapter 18

Kay had been excited since she boarded the space ship. Many things were going through her mind. They would land the next morning and she was looking forward to seeing her sons. She had talked to everyone back home on the space com while she was in space. They were amazed at all the things that were available on board to do. She had told them all about the different programs. Luke went wild, and she did not see much of him the whole trip. Vince was talked into a few things, but preferred to stay in the room and read. He was old-fashioned in that respect. The new route through the second wormhole was used and it took off that extra week.

"Well, we will be landing tomorrow," Kay said as she flopped down on the bed beside Vince while his nose was stuck in the book.

"Yeah." That is all Vince said as he continued to read.

"Don't you get the least bit excited or afraid of new things? I mean how can you sit in here and read the whole time without wanting to do all these programs...and you know, live a little." Kay was talking, but wasn't sure he was listening. She got up and started out the door. She turned around and asked one more time. "Don't you want to come?"

"Kay, I've seen and done all that. I'm tired and just want to read... ok."

"OK, I'll go find Luke," Kay said and went out the door. She did not know why she tried so hard to change Vince. He was who he was, and because of that mindset he made a great rocket engineer. Sometimes she just wanted to see him let go and have some fun. She saw Luke coming toward her at that time.

"Luke, do you want to go to the virtual beach?" Kay asked.

"Not right now. I want to go with my new friend to the circus." He looked over and Ronny came around the corner. Kay did not care for Ronny and neither did Vince, but they let this little friendship form while on board. They figured that once Luke got to Ameriland, he would make new friends.

"Oh, all right. Do you need more tokens?" Kay asked hesitantly.

"No, we have plenty. Well I'll see you later." Luke went on down the hall with Ronny.

Kay went back into the room. Vince had not moved.

"Did you change your mind about doing something?" Vince looked up from his book.

"I just saw Luke. He wanted to go to the circus with Ronny," Kay replied and sat in a chair.

"I don't trust that kid, there is something about him that makes me nervous," Vince said. Kay rolled her eyes.

"Vince, you don't trust any kid. You always think they are up to something."

"They usually are."

"And what do you think this kid is up to, at the ripe old age of 10?" Kay asked.

"Oh, he may have a 10-year-old body, but he knows a lot more then Luke. I prefer to keep Luke innocent for as long as we can," Vince replied.

"Well, maybe this friendship will end with this trip," Kay said, and she hoped she was right.

They were quietly resting when a knock was heard at the door. Kay opened the door and faced one of the on-board patrols.
"Hi. I'm Patrolman Woods. Does this young fellow belong to you?"

"Yes sir. What is the problem?" Kay asked. Vince was behind her at that point.

"Well, nothing real serious. He and another fellow were trying to sneak into the virtual circus. It seems they had no tokens. We will let it pass, but this young fellow better not try it again or it will be more serious next time. You go in and talk to your parents now and no more trouble." The officer went on about his business before Kay or Vince could say anything to him.

"Luke you get in here right now!" Vince was angry and Luke was scared.

"Luke how could you? You stood right in front of me and lied about the tokens." Kay was upset and said the first thing that she thought of.

"Mom, I did not lie about the tokens," Luke said and he pulled out a handful from his pocket. Kay just looked at him with a confused expression.

"So, you just had to see if you could sneak in without getting caught. Oh, let me guess, this was Ronny's idea," Vince said and looked over at Kay. Luke said nothing, because he wasn't going to rat on his new friend.

"Well, you can't hang out with Ronny tonight. We will be in Ameriland in the morning, so that is that," Kay said.

"Luke, go to your room and stay. You can come out to eat and that is all until we land," Vince said. When he was out of the room, Vince turned to Kay.

"Don't say it!" Kay said and put her hand up.

"I was just thinking. I know kids do things and you expect they will get into trouble sometimes, but do our kids have to try every wrong thing that comes along? I just can't figure, we spend years teaching them right from wrong and one little kid comes along and wham... just like that they go for it. What is it about our kids?" Vince was pacing. He got that way when he was upset.

"I don't think it is just our kids. I will admit our boys have tried everything, and we are still not finished. They seem to settle down the older they get. They will remember what they have been taught. I just worry about their safety until they grow up."

"They have been protected so far with our prayers and guidance. Nothing too serious has happened." Vince was a little calmer. Vince and Kay were like that, they were hardly ever upset at the same time. When one was upset the other could calm the situation down.

The next morning was the anticipated landing. Kay and Vince had stored all of the furniture in their storage unit back home, so they had very few belongings on board. The new home was furnished with all the essential things. This move was not a permanent one and they didn't worry about surrounding themselves with the things from back on Earth. A few crates were down in the baggage department, and they carried what they could. They gathered in the main seating area for landing. There was a good view and it was a clear day.

The landing was a little bumpy due to some air disturbance, but all went well. Kay immediately noticed the beauty of the terrain, and Luke noticed the different animals wandering the fields. Vince, however, was studying the rocket ships that were scattered around. Each was in his own train of thought as they entered the space station.

"Wow, hey Luke, did you see those big green birds fly over?" It was Ronnie who broke the silence as he raced up behind them. Vince rolled his eyes at Kay. Kay warned him with her eyes not to make a negative comment, since Ronnie's parents had caught up with them.

"Hi, you must be the parents of this fine young man. Ronnie has been happy to have a friend already in our new world." Mr. Chiles stuck out his hand to Vince. Vince slightly smiled at the red curly haired pudgy version of his son. Mrs. Chiles also greeted them.

"Do you have someone here to meet you?" Mrs. Chiles asked Kay.

"Yes, someone from Lockheed will be here and hopefully our two older sons will be here," Kay replied.

"Oh your sons have already made the trip?" Mrs. Chiles asked fishing for more information. Kay wanted to talk as little as possible, because she wanted to get inside to greet her sons.

"They have been here. They are Ameriland students," Kay said and spotted a familiar face in the crowd.

"They must be smart kids to be in Ameriland School," Mrs. Chiles said. Kay said a quick, "nice to meet you," and scooted toward the crowd. The boys were there and coming toward them. They were a wonderful sight and they all hugged.

"Hello Vince, I almost missed you in this crowd." It was Tom Holmes from Lockheed. Kay and Vince turned around to talk to him about the plans to get to their new home. They were to take a company canal boat to the dock that leads to the new community. When they arrived at the dock there would be a hover bus to take them to the house. Kay thought this sounded exciting, just going to the house, and she looked around for Luke to tell him about it. Reeny had him upside down and Max was tickling him. He was laughing and screaming at the same time.

"Vince, tell the brothers to stop torturing Luke!" Kay pleaded with Vince.

"Boys, we have to be on our way. Put your brother down, there will be plenty of torture time later," Vince said and Tom laughed.

"Well, this way. Everyone to the Canal!" Tom said.

"Uh, Dad. Can I speak to you?" Reeny asked his dad in a low voice. Vince went over to the side with Reeny.

"What's up?" Vince asked when they were away from the others.

"Dad, I have my own craft. I don't want Mom upset, so that is why I didn't tell you earlier on the space com calls." Reeny was still keeping his voice low.

"Reeny how can you afford a craft..." Vince started the question, but Kay came up.

"Honey, Tom said the canal boat is waiting. What is wrong?" Kay asked suspiciously.

"Nothing Mom. Max and I have a way to get to the house. We will meet you there,"

Reeny quickly said, because Max walked up at that time.

"All right, we will talk to you later then," Vince said and took Kay's arm and steered her toward Tom.

"What was that all about?" Kay asked.

"Everything is fine. We will hash it out tonight." Kay did not look satisfied.

"Honey the kids have been on their own, sort of, for a while now. They have their ways of getting around and doing things for themselves. We will catch up to them later." Kay knew the tone of voice Vince was using meant a final answer for now. She would find out later what was going on.

They finally arrived at their new home and Kay could not believe what she was seeing. The house was beautiful and the gardens were breathtaking. She had never lived in such a wonderful place. The view over the canal was like a window into paradise.

"Are you sure this is our place?" Kay asked Tom.

"This is it. There are really not too many ugly places on Ameriland," Tom replied.

"Well, let's go in," Vince said, but everyone stopped when they heard a loud roar coming up the hill.

"Honey what is that noise?" Kay asked Vince, and they all were looking down the hill.

The noise was louder as the raggedy craft floated, kind of, up the hill. It came to a halt and fell to the ground with a thud. Kay grabbed Luke with one hand and Vince with the other. Vince knew who would get out of the craft. It could only be Reeny and Max. When the dirt settled and the doors popped open, the boys got out all smiles.

"What do you think? It needs work, but it gets me where I'm going," Reeny was saying as he came toward them. Vince went over to inspect the craft. Kay knew now what the secret was about earlier.

"Reeny how did you get a craft? They can be dangerous, even with all the safety features." Kay was scolding.

"Mom, I have had this craft for a few weeks, nothing bad has happened," Reeny said.

"Well, I hope you did not give too much for it," Vince was saying and still inspecting the craft. "Just how did you buy it?"

"That is another thing I needed to tell you. I have a job," Reeny said proudly.

"The school let you get a job, Reeny, what about your studies?" Kay asked.

"Honey, let's talk about this later. We need to let Tom show us the house and tell us some things we need to know. I'm sure he has to get back to his family," Vince was saying.

Luke ran off somewhere to explore and everyone else went into the house. It was a big home. It had large rooms and open spaces. Kay was pleased and the boys liked the place. They had come earlier to look at the house but could not get in. When they told Kay that, it explained how they knew how to get there. Supper that night would be a catching up time. Kay wanted to know what her sons were up to on a daily basis, but something else told her that she may not really want to know.

They ordered dinner from the spacecom system. Vince usually liked to cook the old-fashioned way, but they were too hungry to wait. While they were eating they talked. Kay noticed when they ate together, she could find out a lot about what was going on with the family. It seemed Luke had found a stream full of new, exciting creatures to study. She knew he would spend his entire school vacation scrounging the surrounding area. Kay expressed a certain concern about his safety and the idea of running afoul of something unknown that could hurt him. The boys all laughed because their mom had such an imagination about what could happen to them. Vince assured her he would find out if there was anything dangerous around.

The subject finally fell to the craft Reeny had purchased. Reeny told his reason why he worked and had a job. Vince saw the logic in it, but Kay wondered about it. They discussed moving Max and Reeny into their new rooms the next day. Max seemed happy about it and Reeny seemed just to go along with the plans. When they left that evening and Luke was in his room, Kay talked to Vince about it.

"Reeny did not seem happy about moving here. I would think they would be happy to get out of the dorms," Kay contemplated out loud.

"Hon, it is like I said. They have been on their own, in a way, for a while. Reeny is going to find it hardest to live under our rules. He has always been independent," Vince explained.

"But they have very strict rules at the school. It would seem they could have more freedom here," Kay said.

"That would be the way Max would see it, but not Reeny," Vince said as he got into bed. Kay knew as soon as his head hit the pillow he would be asleep, so she did not say anything else about it. She thought about it though and wondered why Reeny was such a puzzle.

"Why didn't you tell them you would be taking the flight school exam this school break?" Max asked Reeny when they were on their way back to the school that night.

"Mom would not be able to handle all that right now. She needs to get adjusted to her new home and planet. If she knew I would not be living with them next school year because I chose to go to flight school, she would be unhappy again. I will move in during school break and then I will tell them when I pass the exam," Reeny said.

"You used the word 'when' you pass the exam, not 'if' you pass the exam," Max said.

"I know. I will pass that exam, I know that," Reeny said and nothing else on that subject was discussed between them that night. Reeny's thoughts were back on Karu, who had not been able to make the trip to the station. Scout had stayed with Karu.

The boys moved all their belongings in the next day. They settled into a normal family life, at least as normal a life as one can have on another planet. Kay found neighbor friends and Vince moved into the daily routine of his new job smoothly. Luke had a lot of freedom on his break and went for it full blast. He knew he would be in a new school soon and it was scary. It was a small public school with many diverse children from Russo and America. Luke would get special help because of his dyslexia. Kay had spoke several times with the special ed teachers and felt satisfied that he would be taken care of. They were going to put him on a program during the break to get him ready, and Kay wondered if this would work when his mind was on play.

It would be summer back in America. Summer break for school had become popular again after many experimental ways of breaking up the school year had been tried. Ameriland had adopted the same time frame, since there were many Americans in the schools here and most American traditions were kept. There was no changing of the seasons to tell them it was summer, but everyone treated it the same as he would if he were on Earth in America. The lazy summer days passed by as Max and Reeny made their Mom happy by being good for a change. The only thing that upset Kay was Reeny's job. She worried about his safety in town and he got in late. She did not go to sleep until she heard the roar of that machine coming up the hill.

Chapter 19

Reeny came in excited one day and waved a piece of paper. Kay looked around to see what the commotion was. She had been trying to cook an old-fashioned dinner, but Vince was the better cook. She was determined to make a meal that came out great. She had flour all over her when Reeny gave her a hug of delight.

"Reeny what is all the excitement about?" Kay asked.

"I got in, Mom! I should have let you know what was going on. I just did not want you unhappy any longer then you needed to be," Reeny started explaining.

"What are you talking about?" Kay asked, wiping her hands on a towel. Reeny observed his mom and what she was doing.

"Mom, are you trying to cook again? Why do you do this to yourself? You should just order over the com line instead. If you want home cooked, Dad likes to do this," Reeny said and Kay looked unhappy.

"Mom, I'm sorry for hurting your feelings," Reeny said when he realized what he had done.

"That is all right. You see, for the first time since you were babies, I'm going to be home for a while. I thought I could learn some cooking, and maybe do some writing. I will try to get a teaching job here in another year, but in the meantime, I could use this time wisely. Even when I was at home when you were babies, I didn't get a chance to learn how to cook because your dad would come home and take over the kitchen." Reeny was beginning to understand his mom a little and nodded his head.

"So, tell me what is so exciting." Kay observed the paper in Reeny's hand.

"Oh, Mom. I uh took the exam to get into flight school and, well, I passed. There is Dad coming in and I'll explain more to you both," Reeny said as he watched his dad coming up the hill from the canal.

When Vince came in and greetings were made, Reeny was ready to explain to his parents what he had been up to.

"I didn't know you could get into flight school at seventeen," Kay said when Reeny finished his rehearsed speech to his parents.

"Yes you can get into flight school if you pass that exam. Reeny, I heard that not too many students passed it even at eighteen. You have done well to have passed it the first time," Vince said in a very proud voice.

"Jon passed it too, and Scout. We were the only ones this year to get in," Reeny said.

"Jon and Scout too? Wow that is good!" Vince said.

"What does this mean exactly?" Kay asked.

"Mom, I'll have to move into the dorms at the flight school this coming school year," Reeny said.

"Oh Reeny, you have always tried to grow up too fast. Now you are going to miss all your last year in Ameriland and all those things they get to do the last year. What about all the activities and the dances? What about the graduation ceremony?" Kay asked.

"Mom, you know I don't care about all of that," Reeny said.

"You might one day wish you had not jumped ahead of time," Kay said, but she knew Reeny would not change his mind. He was going to Karu's house to share the news and he had hoped he could beat Scout there. When he went out the door and the craft noise echoed down the hill, Kay turned to Vince.

"Why does he do this? He has never wanted to be a kid. He has so much in front of him and time to be an adult, why does he push himself? First it was the job, now it is this school. This could put him into a war," Kay said.

"I know. I hope he doesn't regret it, but not too many students get into flight school at any age. It is amazing that he got in. Don't worry too much, if there is a war, he will be ahead of the game. Better to be in school, then to be called up and start at the bottom. The school is right next to Lockheed, so it is not far. He'll be fine," Vince said.

"Well I really am all right for some reason. I had hoped he would live here longer, but that is the way it is. Will it be dangerous at all?" Kay asked.

"No, they have a lot of training. They are in the virtual ships a long time before they are ready to fly for real. This will be good for him," Vince reassured Kay. Kay really was at peace with all of it.

The school break moved on and the boys all turned a year older. Reeny at seventeen was ready to go to flight school. Max at fifteen was still finding his way, and sometimes he found trouble. Luke at ten was growing and learning many new things. Kay was learning to cook and anticipated the arrival of Vince's mom. Kay admired Vince's mom, she wasn't afraid to try new things and she was well educated. She was going to be the first of the family to visit. Kay had tried to convince her parents to come with her mother-in-law, but that was too much, they preferred not to venture out of their world. Kay had hoped that with time, her parents would come. She talked to them every week on the com phone. They seem to be handling this move well, better then Kay would have thought.

"Luke what are you doing?" It was Vince's voice and Kay went to investigate. "What was Luke up to now?" Kay mumbled to herself. Luke had the recorder and was walking around the rooms of the house and talking to someone.

"I'm showing Nana the house. She can't come see us now, so I wanted to show her a few neat things," Luke was saying.

"Hey Mom, we did not know Luke had you on the phone. How do you like the tour?" Kay asked referring to Luke's idea of recording the house from room to room.

"Luke is quite a tour guide. I like the house. He even took it outside. What a view!" Kay's mom said.

"Yes it is beautiful, but I miss ya'll," Kay said.

"I know. Has Reeny moved to flight school yet? I wanted to send him a little something."

"Oh, you don't have to do that. He'll be moving next week," Kay replied.

"We are all so proud of him. It is a little scary though when we hear about the Talcots on the news. Does Vince know a little more about the situation?" Kay's mom asked anxiously.

"If he does, he doesn't say much about it," Kay said as Vince entered the room at that time.

"Hi Nana, Luke is trying to get the recorder going upstairs so you can see the rest of the house. Were you talking about me?" Vince asked.

"Vince you are paranoid," Kay said back and continued to talk to her mother about the rest of the family back home. Luke cut in with his pictures of the upstairs, and she let him finish talking to his grandmother. When the "tour" was over, Vince and Kay said good-bye to Nana and reflected on some things that needed to get done. They had to see that Reeny was settled at school and Luke was prepared for his new school. Kay told Vince she was happy his mom was coming, because she would be a big help in these hectic last days of the break.

Kay cried a little when Reeny moved his final things out, but she knew he would be home a lot over the weekends and some evenings. They enrolled Luke and met his teachers. Kay and Vince went to the Ameriland School with Max. They wanted to see the place their boys had been the last few years. It was impressive. They met face to face some of the people at school that they had only talked to over the com phone. When Vince and Kay got back home from the school, Rita, Vince's mom had prepared some food. It was a nice surprise and Luke said he had helped. Kay wondered about that, but enjoyed the moment anyway. Rita had just arrived the day before and already had made a difference in the household. Kay still had so much to do in the house and an extra pair of hands was needed.

"Uno seemed to be nice." Vince broke the silence when they were eating.

"Uno?" Kay asked.

"Yes, you know, the Talcot." Vince said.

"Oh yeah, you know, I don't think I will ever get used to that third eye," Kay said.

"I think Talcots are neat." Luke jumped into the conversation.

"Well, I have yet to meet one," Rita said.

"We can go into town to the pizza shop where Reeny works sometime. There are plenty of Talcots there," Vince said.

"I don't know if he will be able to keep that job and be at flight school. Do you know?" Kay asked.

"I think as time goes by, he will find it hard to keep such a schedule. I don't know the rules about jobs at the school, but they are probably the same as Ameriland," Vince said.

"We know he will try it as long as he can. We do need to go visit him soon. It would be interesting," Rita said.

Rita's visit soon came to an end and it was time to see her off. She promised to come back the next year. Kay had to adjust to being in an empty house for the first time in her life. She had always had children about or she was at work. She used the time to do a lot of things she had always wanted to do, thus began a new phase in her life.

The early months of the school year continued on. Kay found herself listening for the rattle of Reeny's craft. His visits were getting few and far between, and Kay figured this would happen once he got caught up in his new school.

Kay heard the noise of the craft coming up the hill one evening just before Christmas. Vince would be home soon and she thought she had better just order food from the com pantry. Back home the house had pre-stocked items, but here the food was brought to the home pantry via hover trucks. The food was cooked, or not, depending on time. Kay ordered cooked food, because she knew everyone would be hungry soon.

Kay turned around from the com pantry and saw a pretty plant with a beautiful flower blooming on it. She thought Luke had brought it to her so she went to pick it up.

"Mom, don't pick that up!" It was Reeny who had just walked in the door. Kay turned questioningly to Reeny and back to the plant. It gave a squeal and scampered across the counter. Kay gave an equal squeal and jumped.

"What was that?" Kay asked Reeny. Luke had witnessed the last part of the scene and was laughing.

"Mom, it is an Emero," Luke said still amused at his mom's reaction.

"Kay what was the screaming about?" Vince was out of breath from running the rest of the way up the hill. He had heard Kay scream.

"There was an Emero in the house," Reeny said.

"A what?" Vince looked around cautiously.

"It is an Insect. It stings. It not a bad sting, but some people get an allergic reaction from it," Reeny said.

"Well, what does it look like?" Vince was still looking around.

"It looks like a beautiful flower. It was just on the counter as if it had been put there. I was going to pick it up, but Reeny stopped me," Kay said.

"Mom, you have to be careful. Remember to approach anything out of the ordinary with caution," Reeny said.

"Don't worry honey, we will learn," Vince assured Kay when he saw her face.

That evening when Max arrived home from a school game, they all sat down to eat and talk. Kay loved these moments. Reeny informed them he had a girlfriend who was an Amerilander. He wanted permission to bring her over for Christmas. Kay and Vince both agreed, and they were a little surprised. They did not ask Reeny much about it because Reeny would clam up if questioned too much. Max wanted to get a job, but they discouraged him, saying he needed to study more at

school.   Luke had missed a homework
assignment and Vince got on to him about
that. Other than all that news, the rest of the
evening went well and they had many such
evenings after that.

Christmas break came and Reeny was
home for a few days. He told his parents
about flight school. He did not like the class
work and he was anxious to get to the virtual
flying. Vince told him that he would have to
be more patient. Things took time to do, and
he could not just jump into this like he did
everything else.

Reeny picked up Karu Christmas Eve
and arrived at home with a big noise. Kay was
a bit nervous, but she imagined Karu was
even more nervous. The meeting went well
and the conversation was pleasant when they
were eating. Kay and Vince again knew better
then to ask Karu too many questions. They
knew Reeny would not like that so they let the
evening flow. When Reeny left to take Karu
home, Kay and Vince had time to reflect on
the situation and wonder how this would work
out.   They voiced their concerns over the
differences and put in an extra prayer for the
two of them. Kay and Vince were about that
age when they met and starting dating. That
gave Kay a lot to think about that night when

the house was quiet and Vince was lightly snoring away.

The days fell into what would have been spring on Earth. Kay missed the changing seasons as she moved about in her world. She had started drawing again and she wrote a little poetry now and again. Her writing was more for therapy than anything else. It calmed her down in the troubled times. The news again was full of stories of Russo and the uprisings there. The Canots had sided with the Talcots over the land issues. That made half of Russo against the other half. The question remained if and when this conflict would spill over into Ameriland.

The news reached America and Kay received concerned com calls from those back home. Some travel to Ameriland had been suspended until things could be sorted out. It may have been an over-reaction to things, but to Kay it seemed reasonable. She did not want to see anyone in any danger. The ships were easy targets and no one wanted to provide an easy target right now.

Reeny was upset when he came home one afternoon. Kay asked what was wrong and he turned on the news. There had been a bomb set off in the city and it had destroyed a building and killed an undetermined number of people. Vince came home with the same news.

"Kay, this happens everywhere. In America this same thing is happening. People are taking sides and making statements. There are people who think we should give part of Ameriland away to the Talcots. It just is not that simple. The Talcots have had a bad time in the past, but the way they are going about this is wrong. Killing innocent people does not help their cause. Do you know that most of those people killed were Americans? They were of all nationalities, which did not set well with most of America. We are going to be pulled into this conflict. We have been told that we have the contract to make more of those war ships. That ought to tell you something of what to expect."

"It scares me because of the boys," Kay said.

"I know." That is all Vince could say. Reeny would be eighteen soon and right in the middle of this war. Max would be right after him if it continued. He knew his boys would do what they had to do, and he was proud of them. Max had been talking about going to flight school, if he could get in.

There were more bombs going off throughout the planet, but so far it was just a few individuals who were involved. It was hard to punish them, since they went into hiding. A big part of Ameriland was unsettled and places to hide were plentiful. Everyone tried to go about his daily business and not give in to these threats. Life became less simple than it had been before, and adjustments in "paradise" had to be made.

Chapter 20

"Scout, cover me! Scout, what are you doing?" There was fire coming out from the ship Reeny was in and he was going down. The ground was getting closer and closer and everything shut off. Reeny yanked his helmet off and popped open the virtual ship's door.

"Scout what were you thinking about? I just got killed again!" Reeny fussed at Scout who had emerged from her ship. She was in a huff too. This had been a tough program and frustrations were high.

"Calm down Reeny, it was just as much my fault," Jon said when he pulled off his helmet and he too stepped out of his ship.

"No it wasn't, you had the enemy at your back door. Scout was free to fire," Reeny said looking over at Scout.

"Well, I've had enough. I have to go. We've done this program to death," Scout said.

"You've got that right," Reeny spoke to her as she left the virtual room.

"Reeny, don't be so hard on her. She is one of the best," Jon said.

"What good is the best, if we are dead?" Reeny said and stomped out of the room. Jon shook his head and decided to go see Hannah. She could always make him feel better.

Reeny had turned eighteen that summer and was looking forward to getting into the real ships. If they could master all the levels in the virtual ships, they could move on to the real ships that were tested over a small moon nearby. They landed and practiced their fighting skills there. Reeny had been to the moon "Eli" many times to observe, and he was getting restless again. Reeny always wanted to push the process. Scout, on the other hand, took her time and Jon went along. They had to be together because that is how it was set. It was like the Earth geese, a "v" shape at all times and each looking out for the others. He had to bring his geese to par quickly, but he did not know what drove him so much.

Reeny went home that evening after giving Karu a com call. He felt the need to get out of the school for a few hours. The flight school's work load was getting heavier and he had to cut back his hours at work. He hoped his mom was cooking. The smell of home made him feel good, and she always had a hug for him. She had mastered some pretty interesting meals, and she actually was getting pretty good in the kitchen.

Max seemed abnormally happy and Reeny wondered what was up.

"What are you high on?" Reeny asked.

"Nothing man, I don't take that stuff. Can't a guy just be happy?" Max asked and shoved Reeny. This of course resulted in some more shoving until Kay told them to stop. Reeny wasn't going to quit there, so Luke looked like an easy target. He had Luke upside down and screaming before long.

"Reeny, what is wrong with you this evening? Leave your brothers alone!" Kay said.

"How is school Reeny?" Vince asked, guessing this might be the cause of the aggressive spurt Reeny was showing.

"Harder. I want to get into the real ships. We can't seem to get past level 8. We have to get to level 10 before we can get into them," Reeny said.

"Reeny you are just eighteen. What is the average age of the students in the ships flying on Eli?" Vince asked.

"I don't know, maybe twenty two or so," Reeny replied.

"What is your hurry son?" Vince asked.

"I don't know that either, I just know I need to do this."

"It is good to have goals Reeny, but you are young and you need to have a good time while you can. There is plenty of time to grow up," Kay said and Reeny rolled his eyes.

"Your mom is right. Most of the students stay in the virtual ships two years or more. There is no need to work yourself up to such frustrating levels. We worry about your health. You have to stay in good health or all of it will be for nothing," Vince said.

Max had been waiting for the right time for his news. It wasn't the right time, but he couldn't hold it back any longer.

"Dad, you know the junior program the flight school has started?" Max asked.

"Oh yes, the program where some of the Ameriland students can take virtual flying lessons at the flight school," Vince said. Reeny did not like where this conversation was going.

"You are not thinking about doing that are you?" Reeny questioned his brother.

"I'm not only thinking about it, but I got in. There were just a few available spots and I was chosen. I found out today," Max said proudly.

"That is great Max, we are proud of you," Vince said as Reeny was looking a bit put out and moaning.

"What is the matter Reeny? Is it your stomach again?" Kay asked.

"No Mom, it is just that we are going to be in charge of these 'characters' when they arrive at the school. Mom, Max won't mind me! This is not good. Can't you find something else to do?" Reeny asked Max.

"Now Reeny, I'm sure Max sees the seriousness of this and will take it so," Vince said.

"Max, this is a good opportunity, do not blow it by messing around," Kay said.

"I'm not Mom, I'll behave," Max said. Everyone was talking about other things finally, but Reeny's head hurt. This had not been a good visit.

"Why did they decide to have this 'junior' program anyway? Does anyone know?" Cole asked. He was one of the flight school students standing around the virtual deck.

"It is supposed to get interest up in joining the military after they graduate from Ameriland. They have many students going into exploration, but very few are interested in flight school," someone answered.

"We have never taken a lot of students anyway."

"They are upping the enrollment due to the circumstances with Russo. We are going to need more students if we go to war soon."

"Well here they come, those little juniors from Ameriland!" The students were walking into the first day on the virtual deck of the flight school. They looked a little excited and a lot afraid when they encountered the older students. A stare-down began, but the officers quickly took charge of the matter. The flight school students were briefed as to their responsibility to these young students, and how they were supposed to be examples. Cole whispered to those around him, "Can someone sing 'Bring in the Clowns'?'" And with that a few giggles erupted. The officer speaking quickly said, "Did everyone hear that we are to be examples?" The officer stared at the group that had laughed and they were silent.

"Now today is just an introduction and for you to get to know which junior you will be in charge of. The names are posted on the board. So people, find your charge. Remember you will see these students twice a week for an hour, and you will need to sign the schedule." With that they were dismissed and there was immediate noise and commotion. Reeny found his name, and his worst fears were realized. He, Scout and Jon were in charge of the trio Max, Summer Faye and Larry. He put his head up against the wall.

"Hey dude, you are going to be in charge of us. That is smooth. Hey, do we get new uniforms?" Larry was putting his hand out to Reeny in greeting. Larry's dark face was brightened with his white toothy smile. Reeny slowly turned around and shook Larry's hand. Reeny gave him a half grin.

"It is not my fault, Reeny." Max came up from behind Larry. Summer Faye was standing nearby, taking it all in.

"Well, I guess we are stuck with you," Reeny said as Jon and Scout came over.

"This will be fun," Scout said.

"I hear Larry is a cutup," Jon said, when they walked away from the others.

"Yeah, I can already tell." They looked over to find him joking and causing the others around him to laugh.

"It is only two hours a week. How much trouble can they be?" Jon asked.

Max, Summer Faye and Larry met with their mentors each week. The first days were spent getting to know the in's and out's of the virtual deck and the ships.

"Hey man, what is this?" Larry asked as he touched a bright red button. Everything went dark and unfamiliar. Stars were everywhere. "Dude, cool, what virtual place is this?"

"Larry, do not push the buttons. This is a place called Odula. There are many such simulated places. Any place that is on the map can be called up. Do not program anything without permission. Got it, dude?" Reeny said firmly to Larry. Larry gave him his big grin.

The group learned quickly, to Reeny's surprise. They were going to have a go in the virtual ships the following week. They were nervous and excited. Reeny remembered his own excitement with the program and forgave their restlessness. Max had been a surprise. He had turned out to be cooperative and a good student.

Chapter 21

"I just can't believe Christmas is here already." Kay was talking to her mom on the computer phone.

"How are the boys? Are they getting along now that Max is taking a class at Reeny's school?" Kay's mom asked.

"Yes, they are getting along better than ever. Reeny has really done well at the school. He will be one of the younger officers. I guess he will be flying the real ships within this year. He will be only nineteen. The talk of war scares me. What does the news tell you at home? Kay asked.

"Oh it is always the same. I worry about the small attacks here and there on Ameriland. Are you sure you are safe?"

"Yes Mom, if we have fighting here, it would be over the disputed territory. It is far away from us," Kay reassured her mom.

"Is Reeny still serious about that little Amerilander. What is her name?"

"Yes, I guess he is as serious as any 'almost' nineteen-year-old could be. Her name is Karu. We will be going to have Christmas

Eve at their house. It will be interesting. I don't know if this means Reeny is more serious then I think."

"They are growing up. All my grandchildren are growing up fast. I can't believe I have great-grandchildren." Kay's mom was getting teary.

"I know mom, I guess you will be getting together at Christmas, like always," Kay said and thinking that this would be the second Christmas she had missed with the family.

"Yes we will, but I want a computer call when everyone is over here."

"You will get it. I guess I had better go. Everyone is eating here tonight including Karu. She doesn't talk much and it is hard to get to know her. I just don't know what to think of this situation. It would be hard to marry an Amerilander with all the cultural differences. I don't know if Reeny has given all this much thought," Kay said.

"They are still young, and kids today don't get serious this young usually. He could meet a lot of girls between now and the time to settle down," Kay's mom said.

"I guess you are right, but you know Reeny. He grows up fast and it would not surprise me if he got married young." Kay's mom nodded, knowing her daughter was right. Reeny was like that.

"Good-bye Mom, love ya."

"Love ya too. Tell those boys to call me."

"I will." Kay pushed the off button and she heard the craft rattling up the hill. Reeny had turned the craft over to Max. Reeny wasn't using it much since he quit his job. He had decided to put in more study time at school to advance ahead, and he needed all the time he could get. He seldom went out. Kay worried about his obsession to get ahead. She did not say much to him. Reeny needed to relax and have some fun, while Max needed to get more serious about which direction he needed to go. Kay wondered if they would ever be on an even scale.

Kay looked out of the window and something caught her eye on the craft. It looked strange, and Max had gone to his room, so she went out to investigate. When she got to the craft, she noticed the bumper was tied up with a shoestring. She shook her head and wondered what that was about.

Everyone soon arrived for supper. Karu and Reeny had just arrived when they heard Luke howling upstairs. No one said anything, since they knew Max was the cause of Luke's torture. Kay always let them fight it out unless someone got hurt. There was no more noise and they came bouncing down the stairs. Luke was walking funny, and Vince looked down to see why. Luke's shoestrings were missing and he was flopping around the table to sit down.

"Those are the shoes we just bought you Luke, Where are the shoestrings?" Vince asked as they all were sitting down. Everyone looked at Luke.

"Max stole 'em," Luke said.

"I needed 'em for my date tonight. I can't walk around without shoestrings," Max said. At this point Kay knew where Max's shoestrings were.

"Well let me ask, where might your shoestrings be?" Vince asked annoyed at Max.

"Oh the bumper fell off of that piece of junk outside…" Max started explaining, but Reeny jumped up and looked out of the window.

"Man, what did you do to the craft? You have been dogging it!" Reeny said accusingly.

"I have not. It's falling apart. I'll have to tape it together before long. Anyway I had to use my shoestrings to tie it back on. I couldn't take off otherwise. You should have seen it, the bumper scraping the ground.

Everyone was laughing at school, and Summer Faye was with me. Oh it was embarrassing," Max said and Reeny sat back down glaring at Max.

"Maybe I should take it back to school with me," Reeny said.

"Man, no! I'll fix it, when I get a job and some money," Max said.

"Well, we have not solved Luke's problem. Let's see. What is wrong with this picture? Max dogs his craft out and Luke has to give up his shoestrings. Let me see if I can get this straight, because you know, I'm really trying here. Now you need to go on a date and you need shoestrings. Son, have you heard of a place called a 'store'? They sell lots of things, everything you can think of, and you can even get shoestrings there. Wow, think of that novel idea! And you could have bought rope there and saved your shoestrings," Vince said in a sarcastic voice. He got this way sometimes and the boys did not like it.

"Well, if I had had money that would have been great," Max shot back.

"Son, we can give you money to fix the craft," Kay said.

"Oh no you don't. The deal is, if he wants the craft, he takes care of it. That was what I did. If he can't take care of it, then he will not get to use it," Reeny said.

"Look, let's discuss this later. Luke, say the blessing before everything gets cold," Kay said. Karu was as quiet as usual, speaking when only spoken to. Kay wondered if she would ever get to know this girl. She knew Karu had entered the Ameriland College this year, and tried to get a conversation going about that. It did not work for long, and the boys' noise always overrode the conversations.

"I'm hoping to get to be a flight officer this year. I will be nineteen in the summer and I think they will consider me. I can then go to the space academy on Eli for a few months to train. Of course Scout and Jon would come as the wing men," Reeny said.

"When would you know?" Vince asked.

"I think we can master the rest of the levels by summer break. They would let us know before school starts back up," Reeny said.

"So, you would then go to live on the moon, Eli? How long?" Kay asked. Again she could feel her world being shaken.

"Two years, but Mom, it is only a few days away. I'll come home for a lot of breaks." Reeny knew this was the hard part. Karu said nothing and kept her head down.

"They say the chance of my getting into flight school next year is good. I'm already ahead since I've been taking classes there this year," Max chimed in.

"Yes, then you will be moving to the flight school," Kay said sadly.

"I have been home a lot even when I moved to the flight school. You will see Max more then you want to," Reeny said trying to ease the pain of yet another major change for his mom.

"Yes, I know. I'll be all right," Kay said. The rest of the evening went by quickly, and they all went their separate ways. Vince gave Max some money and told him to take care of the craft's bumper.

On Christmas Eve the family went to Karu's house. Kay told Max and Luke to be on their best behavior. She did not know how this visit would turn out. She prayed for the best.

They were greeted at the door by the butler and shown in. Kay knew Karu's parents were well off, but she had not realized to what extent "well off" meant. They looked around with amazement at the house. They were greeted by Karu's mom, Arin. Light conversation flowed, and Karu's dad, Gar, entered the room. They all talked for a while and were shown to the table for dinner.

It was very traditional. Some dishes Kay did not recognize, but all of it was good. Some Christmas decorations filled the room, and a version of a Christmas tree was displayed in the large living area. If an Amerilander chose the traditional Earth tree, it was artificial. The trees here were more tropical. The tree displayed was the traditional live Ameriland Ola. It had large leaves and a fruity smell. Kay thought it was nice. Kay thought about the artificial fur tree back at their home and thought maybe one Christmas they could try an Ameriland tree.

The parents watched Reeny and Karu step out into the gardens together and continued small talk. Nothing deep was exchanged between them. They felt safe that way, but talk of the trouble with the Talcots came into the conversation. Reeny's future came up and there was talk of his leaving for Eli. Kay felt that they wanted to say more about the two young people outside as they gazed that way every now and again.

"I have a feeling we are being watched. Can we move on farther in the garden? Reeny asked.

"Well not too far, or they will send out a search party," Karu said. They walked a while and talked until Reeny stopped and looked serious.

"Karu, I have my flight ring. I would like to give it to you as a sign of pre-engagement. Would you take it and wear it?" Reeny asked a bit awkwardly. He was afraid of what he might hear.

"Oh Reeny, I know this means a lot. I do want to wear it and all... but my parents will be upset. They are upset enough these days about the uprisings. I don't know Reeny..." she stopped talking because at that point Reeny reached over and kissed her. "Reeny what are we going to do?" Karu said as Reeny continued to hug her.

"It will work out. I'll be gone to Eli for two years. I'll visit when I can. I just...I just wanted you to keep my ring. Will you be here when I return? Will you promise to wait for me?" Reeny asked.

"I promise. I'll do what I can with Mom and Dad. I will keep the ring a secret for a while. Reeny you will come back won't you?" Karu asked.

"Of course, don't I always? You know you've tried to get rid of me and it doesn't work." With that they both laughed and they heard their names being called. Moments in one's life have a way of changing destiny forever, and this had been one of those moments for Karu and Reeny. They had stepped into the gardens, two kids in love; they stepped out of the gardens, two adults committed to each other for life.

"Did you program the flight for the guys?" Reeny asked Scout.

"Sure did. You know that Summer Faye is getting a little too uppity. I think she needs a lesson," Scout said.

"Oh, she is just happy they all passed the exam and will enter this school next year. She'll calm down. It's a hard road. You should know," Reeny said. "Here they come now, right on time."

"Man, I am ready for my first virtual flight!" Larry came bouncing in. They all seemed excited, slapping each other on the back.

"Ok, get in Summer Faye, Larry and Max. We are ready to go," Reeny said. Scout had a devious look on her face. Reeny looked at her, puzzled. He had seen this look many times. She was up to something. The program started running through the mountains and valleys as planned. The trio was doing a super job. Then the three began to notice snow showers through the virtual cockpit window.

"Hey, what's this?" Larry asked as he looked over into the ship Max was in. Max looked over to check out Summer Faye. She was in the other ship to his right.

"This is called snow, Larry," Summer Faye answered in a sarcastic way.

"I know, but what are we flying in it for? I mean I did not know this would be part of the program," Larry said.

"Well, it may be a test. Let's keep going," Max said. Soon, they could not see anything and they were using the instruments. It was a disaster. Max plowed into a mountain. Summer Faye's ship went down, and Larry followed Max's fate. Summer Faye had by this time guessed who was responsible for their plight. She popped open her ship and threw off her helmet. She was fussing with a string of Spanish and English words coming out of her at a rapid rate. She was up in Scout's face.

"Excuse me Summer Faye, you forget I speak Spanish...fluently." Scout was nose to nose with Summer Faye. Summer Faye was ready to say more. "Stand back Summer Faye, you are speaking to a flight officer," Scout said.

"I am not a student here yet, and you are just my 'mentor.' Remember?" Summer Faye had Scout on that one.

"Yeah you two gonna fight?" It was Larry, looking for excitement.

"No, you all are dismissed. Summer Faye, go cool off," Reeny said.

"I think we done cooled off enough," Larry said looking back at the snow still lingering around the floor of the virtual landing.

"Let's go Larry," Max said. He did not want to argue today. The three headed out and Max said. "I think we did good on that program." And they were slapping each other in approval.

"Don't say it. I was wrong. It was one of my moments," Scout said.

"You are a flight officer now Scout, you need to act like one," Reeny said and left the room for Scout to reprogram the computer.

Chapter 22

The worst fears had finally set themselves at Amerilands peaceful doors. The Talcots had arrived in war ships and were wreaking havoc on the northern part of the planet called Cavhill by the early American settlers. Those settlers had been there after the Talcots left hundreds of years before. They had mined the area for the rich minerals used throughout the galaxy. They had "carved out" their livings, literally, generation after generation. Now they were being driven out of their homes, killed and tortured.

War was declared. Americans were called up. Russos that were against the Talcots were called to fight. Everything had changed for three worlds of people. Some Canots were fighting with the Talcots. In Ameriland, where they had lived together in peace for a long time, confusion reigned.

Word of war soon reached the moon Eli and Reeny realized what this meant to all of them. He had talked to his mom, who was surprisingly calm. His dad was matter-of-fact. Luke hardly could grasp it at his age, and Max was sorry he was only one year into flight school.

"People, listen up, we have a situation here that requires our best." This was coming from Officer Kelly. "American ships are on their way, but in the meantime, we are needed to bust a target in the Cavhill territory. The caves and mountains are so close together that our 'birds' are the only ones that would be able to get a shot at them." He pushed a button on the desk and up popped a hologram of Cavhill. He zoomed in on a particularly large cave set in the side of one of the tallest mountains. "This is where they have a strong operation, right here in this cave. We need to take them out. If we can cripple them until our forces arrive, we will keep ahead of them. This requires our best shots. We will practice this virtually and in the air for a couple of days. When we find our best three flyers, we take off for our target. Got that? We start today. Move it!" With that they all scrambled to get in position.

"Reeny, do you read? What is wrong with Tera, we are getting no response...repeat...we are getting no response." Officer Kelly was trying to reach one of his own favorite flyers. She had been an asset to the team and had been sent up with Reeny for a practice run.

"Officer Kelly... we ran into some space debris. Tera's ship took a beating Sir. I'm closing in on her to get a closer look. Sir, she seems unconscious. I can get the space cable out to her from my ship and latch onto her, but I'm taking it hard with the flying debris," Reeny said.

"Reeny do what you can...repeat...do what you can."

"I'm on it Sir. My cable has been attached..." Noise and static were heard.

"Reeny do you hear me... Reeny..."

"Sir, my cable has become detached. I'm working to get it back. My left wing...hit...repeat...I have hit debris and crippled my left wing."

"Get another bird up there quickly!" Officer Kelly cried out. Scout and Jon ran to get in their ships without hesitation. When they arrived on the scene, the debris was just about out of the area. The crippled ships looked as bad as the garbage they had hit. Reeny's cable was attached to Tera's ship and they were limping toward Eli. Reeny's ship was limply making it in.

"Situation under control...Scout and Jon... Just follow me in." Scout and Jon followed closely until Reeny's ship began to lose its balance in space. Scout attached a cable onto Tera's ship and Jon attached another to Reeny's ship and they all came in safely to the landing site. They had the medics get Tera out quickly and check Reeny. Reeny had suffered only bruising, but Tera had head injuries. Word came quickly that her injuries were not life-threatening.

"Well, I think we've found our team. They work well together, not afraid of things and Reeny is our best shot." Officer Kelly addressed Officer Jane Stamos.

"I think you may be right Kelly. When can we get them on the starship for Ameriland?"

"First thing in the morning. Oh by the way, some of our students from the flight school have arrived to observe. Some of them may go on the starship carrying the ships. They can be of some help," Kelly said.

"Good, I'll see to it," Officer Stamos answered.

Reeny, Jon and Scout were briefed on their mission. Not one of them backed away from the task before them. They knew what they had to do and why they were there. They talked little to each other and made preparations in their own ways.

"Hey Reeny!" Reeny turned around and could not believe his eyes. It was Max. Max had been on Eli observing before, but Reeny did not expect to see him at this time.

"Max, I'm glad to see you. Max I'm going on that mission tomorrow and it could be dangerous. I can't let anyone at home know, because it is a secret mission. I'm glad you are here. I want to send a message to Mom and Dad...in case..." Reeny could not finish what he was saying.

"Don't worry Reeny you will make it. You always come through." Max slapped his older brother's back. "I'm going on the starship that is carrying the birds and ya'll tomorrow," Max said.

"Max, I don't know if that is a good idea. Can't they get someone else?"

"No way, I'm going," Max said. They both walked in silence.

Here they stood at the starship window, each wondering how they got to be here. Max was looking over Reeny's shoulder and finally the silence was broken.

"Make sure that you are the one to tell Mom and Dad, if things go wrong," Reeny said.

"Don't worry Ren. It will be fine. You are the best and you have Scout and Jon,"

Max said and put his hand on Reeny's shoulder. Scout and Jon walked up and gazed out of the window.

"It is beautiful. I can't believe we are on this mission. Everything is so peaceful now," Scout said.

"It won't be when we reach Ameriland," Jon said.

"We had better go get some rest, before time," Reeny said and they all agreed.

The three small ships took off out of the starship. Destination, Cavhill.

"Do you read me?" Reeny asked. Scout and Jon responded. The starship was keeping in touch throughout this mission, giving instructions when needed. This was what worried Reeny with Max aboard. He knew he would hear all the exchange.

The small ships were dwarfed in the distance and Max was saying a prayer for his brother. He knew Reeny was saying his own prayers. There was a lot of movement on the starship, as they were preparing to guide the mission and respond with other flyers if needed. Max hoped no one else would be needed, and that Reeny, Scout and Jon would be successful.

"All right we have the target in view." It was Reeny's voice.

"You need to take those birds as far in as you can. I know it will take a quick pull-up out of the hills, but you have done this in the virtual ship many times," Officer Kelly responded.

"Got it!" Reeny said and the others agreed, as they got closer to their prey.

They lowered themselves into the hills. Each hill had large caves, once used for dwellings in the early years. There was movement among the caves now because of the new residents who were hiding in them. Shots were fired at the ships, but the gun power was not reaching, yet. Reeny knew they had the power to bring the birds down and they needed to move quickly.

"I see the main cave," Scout said. "It is ahead of us."

There were sounds above them and they realized it was enemy ships. The older larger ships could not get down into the hills like the smaller ships, but the three knew that they could fire on them.

"Reeny, do you think they will risk firing on us now? They could hit their own comrades," Jon said.

"No, they are waiting until we get out. Be prepared for a fight. We have to try to get our target. Ready with the 'guns'. Take aim!

We have to do this now. Fire!" Reeny yelled out the order. The missiles were headed directly to the target. Reeny was ahead and his missile was going straight for the throat of the cave. Jon and Scout's were headed for the encampments on each side of the cave. They had no time to watch, they had to pull out of the hills before they hit them. When they were out, firing began from the larger enemy ships.

"We are being fired on... repeat, fired on. Do we have back-up?" Reeny was yelling. Max's heart was racing and he wondered about being there to witness this. What would he tell his parents?

"Negative. We are sending back-up now," Officer Kelly said and started barking orders for the other birds to get busy. "I was hoping not to have to send any more of our men. They caught on to the plan quicker then I would have thought." He said this to Officer Stamos, but Max had heard the exchange. Max bit his lip.

"Reeny do you read? Reeny!"...and there was static. It had been Scout.

"Sir, Reeny's ship had been hit. He is going down!" Jon was yelling.

"We are fighting for our lives here, where is our back-up?" Scout was trying to keep a cool head, but was losing it.

"Try to contact Reeny," Officer Kelly said to the young man with the headgear.

"We've lost contact, Sir." The young man looked up in despair. Max ran from the room.

"Reeny do you read? I'm getting no response Jon," Scout said. Help came up from behind them and distracted the ships so Jon and Scout pulled out of the fight.

"We have to go back. We have to help Reeny!" Scout said to Jon. Scout turned back and Jon followed. Firing on the ships had set the enemy back and they were flying away.

"Reeny come in... Reeny!" Nothing but static could be heard. Both Scout and Jon continued to try for a response. They saw the crippled ship below and it appeared to be in one piece.

Reeny heard the pleas, but had been thrown from his ship. He could not move because he was injured. He was cold. He saw an American flag flapping in the wind on the ground near him. With tears streaming down his face, he grabbed the flag and pulled it close to him. He smelled the Ameriland soil on the fabric and looked up into the sky. He could see the two small suns. He wrapped himself up in the flag and called out to God.

"God, let me live. Let me live to fight again. Let me live to see my family again. Reeny began to get weaker, and with a muffled voice said, "God be with me."

Reeny did live to fight again. Reeny did not know at the time, but his action on the Cavhill territory turned the war to favor Ameriland and her allies. America was on a better footing to fight the war to save Ameriland. Reeny, Jon and Scout were heroes.

ISBN 155395757-1

9 781553 957577